PAULINE DEVINE was born in Loughrea, County Galway, and studied for a social science degree in University College Dublin. Later she attended Trinity College and Sydney University, where her subject was education.

She prefers ponies to processors and exhibits Connemara pony Sheeogue, a hardy and sociable soul, who likes winning rosettes and fancies being out in the field with the young horse.

Married, with one daughter, Pauline lives on the borders of Dublin and Kildare, where she looks after her two horses. She is treasurer of her local pony club and an exhibitor and prizewinner at the Kerrygold Dublin Horse Show. She also helps out with hunting and gymkhanas and enjoys going to schools to talk about – ponies and horses.

She has also written *Best Friends,* the first book about Sarah and Bluebell; *Riders by the Grey Lake,* set in her native Galway; *The Hungry Horse* and *King Longbeard.* She was the first writer of children's books to be awarded an Arts Council Bursary.

Pauline Devine

BEST FRIENDS AGAIN

Illustrated by Terry Myler

THE CHILDREN'S PRESS

For
Maria and her grandmother
Ellie Clery

First published 1999 by
The Children's Press
an imprint of Anvil Books
45 Palmerston Road, Dublin 6

2 4 6 5 3 1

© Text Pauline Devine 1999
© Illustrations Terry Myler

ISBN 1 901737 14 4

Typeset by Computertype Limited
Printed by Colour Books Limited

J74811
£3·95

CONTENTS

1 A FAREWELL

Bluebell's big breath warmed the cold air as we trotted along the track. She shot back one ear to listen to me. 'You can't be happy all the time. Things are always changing. Now the sun is shining but soon it might be pouring rain or hailstones. Or we could have a storm or something.'

Through the gap in the trees we saw the strange jeep and horse-box parked in Caseys' driveway. When we came closer, the horse-box gave a lurch and two bug eyes stared out at us through the open side door. Bluebell sniffed with curiosity at Paula's new pony.

'I'm taking him out now.' Paula stepped in and started to unknot the lead rope.

But Bluebell had lost interest. She was looking about for Blackie, her old friend. Nose in the air asking questions, she whizzed round the house and braked outside his stable. Blackie, eager to hack out with us as usual, kicked at the door.

There was a shout from Paula. It was nearly time for Blackie to be taken away but she wanted us to leave first. 'He mightn't load if Bluebell is here.'

I stroked Bluebell's bony face and slowly she obeyed. We had reached the elbow bend near the castle when the horse-box passed. Seeing Blackie's face above the ramp moving away from her, Bluebell whinnied sharply. I patted her but she whinnied again and broke into a fast trot. Back came Blackie's whinny.

We were scooting along the grass verge in pursuit; she can move when she wants to. 'Whoa ... easy, Bluebell ... ' Her skin shook, the leaves shook golden on the beech trees we swept by, coarse grass shook where we trampled it, shook wet and damp in our faces. She and Blackie answered one another and long after the horse-box had disappeared, their whinnies rolled over and back on Tooten Hill and down into the Liffey valley.

Blackie was gone. Bluebell was wasting her time chasing that jeep. One ear shot sideways again, listening to my soft words, and she slowed down.

Before, when Bluebell and I reached this point on the road Blackie would whinny a welcome. Would he ever again nip Bluebell's neck or share her trough or her stable or graze with her on Paula's lawn?

She broke into a trot again. 'Easy pet.' I wiped my face and another thought fizzed up inside me. Blackie was old. He had learned some bad habits like bolting for home and running out at fences.

Salute the magpie for luck.

No matter how Paula tried, from now on he would not improve on his performance with practice as Bluebell would, she being a young pony.

Slow down, driver. Thanks.

And he would never again be fit for a cross-country course, never mind a day's hunting over big ditches and drains. He would not survive, probably fall into a river and drown. The last cross-country had shown that clearly.

'Bluebell, it's only a frog. Trot on.' We veered out of its path.

Blackie's digestion was breaking down too. A few weeks ago the vet said Paula should allow him out on grass for only two hours a day or he'd be airborne – he could even explode with all the trapped air in his stomach. Yes. It was time the old pony took it easy; Paula's little cousins might learn how to ride on him.

Grabbing at a wild plum I accidentally kicked Bluebell and she jumped forward beneath me. Now Paula had a new horse and Bluebell would have a new friend to match her endurance and speed. I patted her sturdy neck. I talk and she listens. I tell her everything, she's a great listener; see ... she bends her neck around like a hair-band and nods her head at me.

To our left is Banshee Hill with its flowering furze bushes and on the right is Tooten Hill. Nearly every day I ride through the nape of those hills. They stay as they are forever. But people and ponies are different; they come and go. I've learned this from my once best friend Babs and from Paula, who is now my best friend. And ponies too come and go. What would happen when Bluebell was Blackie's age? I put the thought away.

Leaning forward by the side of Bluebell's neck, I whispered another thing. Something good always happens. And it was going to be something wonderful. The grass lit up, soaking up light from the evening sun. Bluebell's mane lit up and red berries winked and glistened above and below us in the hedges and ditches as we hopped in, over and out.

Bluebell loves these rough fields. She is a young pony, made for cross-country. This I knew as we raced along. Yes, when I learned to press the right buttons Bluebell could really be very good on Hunter Trials – that first one wasn't a fair test. It was just a hiccup, a bad day that was not likely to happen again.

Setting off for New Ross at dawn that sunny morning for the Inter-Schools Hunter Trials, the lorry powering us along, I agreed with Paula that our ponies could possibly do it. Trevor was punching the air with his fist and shouting Yeah and Niall shook his head so that his thatch of hair flapped and we all laughed when he said we shouldn't be too cocky – even if we were the best team.

In a hollow between two mountains, the cross-country course stretched over ploughed fields with a river snaking around. After walking it no one said a lot.

But we stopped arguing about which one of us should get to bring the trophy in for school assembly on Monday.

It didn't look as if we'd have the trophy. The fences were big and take-off dodgy, the ground softening in the light rain. And yet I thought there was the chance that Bluebell might rise to them.

Then came the torrents of wet and wind that churned up fields and valley, turning them into a lake of creamy mud.

On the programme, we were listed as team 101, one hundred teams to start before us at ninety-second intervals. But with the huge numbers pulling out of the competition, our team was called suddenly. Trevor had to call off because his pony went lame, so Paula, on Blackie, had to take his place. We were freezing and feeling miserable. Couldn't see, ponies and riders vanishing ahead of us in the rain into that lake of whipped cream.

Bluebell nervously jumped the first obstacle, a fallen tree. Next some rotting bales, then the gate. Getting braver and braver as we went on, until the disastrous three refusals at the water jump and elimination. Humiliating.

I remembered the stone-faced bank of that water jump – a river in flood. Nothing short of an explosion would move Bluebell forward over that river. Even Dad failed where he never failed before, the branch of a thorn bush jammed against her tail end. She would have staged a sit-down on the bank if he'd pushed any further.

Next memory was Blackie wading chest-high in the water and Paula being swept under.

Yes, the Trials were a serious washout, as Trevor said. Looking back I could see that Bluebell was too green then for that slippery course – it was like a scene from the film *Waterworld*.

Starting off for home, the whole team was grumpy, even Niall, usually so cheerful. But after we stopped at the Road Runner Diner and tasted those curried chips we cheered up and laughed so much the owner thought we were the winners. Trevor was really proud of his steaming dirty All-Blacks rugby t-shirt.

At school, Katie and Babs teased that the team was

eliminated because of Bluebell, that she was a problem pony. But it wasn't just Bluebell. We would have been disqualified anyhow after Paula's fall. And there was a query that Teabag might have run out on Niall at the finishing line.

One day soon Bluebell would scoop the top award – given the right conditions.

'Whoa.' We were back out on the road and close to home. I got down to let Bluebell cool off and led her the rest of the way. We walked along together.

Across from our entrance gate, the evening sun threw a long shadow on to the road. A girl on a horse. She turned her head quickly and looked hard at me.

'Miranda ... Hi!' I was totally unprepared.

Without answering, she clipped her mobile phone back into place and swung her horse out of the gateway. I

watched them trot down the hill. They turned off the road at the new sign for Mrs Montgomery's Riding Centre.

Last summer, at Pony Camp, Miranda came to Bluebell's rescue when she was being kicked by other ponies. That was the first time I met her. After that, we'd bumped into each other at a few horsy activities. Then she'd started working at the riding centre at weekends, preparing for her Pony Club B-Test – the practical part, to do with care and working of a pony. When I helped out there, we sometimes ended up doing chores together and each time she acted the same way. She was polite. Too polite. All she ever said were little things like, 'You have to throw the manure up there and then flatten it out.' Or, 'You can't feed him unsoaked hay – it'll give him a cough.' Or, 'You've dropped half the muck.' Otherwise she never spoke to me. And always that hard stare.

She was much nicer to Paula. This was puzzling because Paula told me how she'd ask about Bluebell and me, even about my mam and dad.

Now that I was back at school, I didn't see much of her. What was she doing in our gateway? Possibly taking a call on her mobile.

Bono, my labrador, scooted up the driveway before us.

Mam would want to hear about Paula's new horse.

2 PAULA'S NEW HORSE

A sackload of empty horse and pony-nut bags, old stable rubbers and torn towels rested at the back door. Mam was in mucking-out mood. I slipped into the kitchen and went to the fridge for some juice – my boots weren't that muddy anyway.

'Mam, is my dinner ready? Paula will be here shortly. She's got her new pony.'

I stopped. Mam was seated in a chair in the study, which is off the kitchen, and she was gazing at the phone in her hand. Beside her, the floor mop lay on the half-washed tiles.

'Mam, what's the matter? Was it another one of those funny calls? Was it that woman who rings and puts the phone down? Hey, Mam,' finally getting her attention by waving my hand up and down before her eyes. She blinked.

'Are you expecting someone?'

She looked as if I had asked her to go on a roller-coaster ride. It was weird. She scared me for a moment.

I picked up the mop. 'Mam ... are we expecting visitors? Who's coming?'

'Coming?' Again that look.

' What's with all the cleaning?'

'Cleaning?' She stared out of the window for a few moments. Then she said absent-mindedly, as if she had forgotten all about them until now, 'Auntie Gweena and Uncle Sam. They'll be staying tonight. They rang earlier.'

'Great!' So this was what the fuss was about. I asked about Gweena's champion hunter, Strike, and where they'd be stabling him but Mam didn't seem to hear.

Tracking over the wet tiles after her: 'Mam, could I go hunting? Our chef d'equipe said it would improve Bluebell's courage and make her more adventurous. It's what she needs.'

'That's wonderful ... '

She mustn't have heard me. 'Hunting would be very good experience for our next cross-country. I don't want the same thing to happen as last time ... '

I had her attention now. 'You and your pony are not experienced enough yet.'

'Well, how are we to get experience if we don't go hunting?'

She didn't answer. She was staring into space again.

'Yum, cheese sauce.'

A stream of it hit the plate. 'Mam, you've made custard instead of cheese sauce!'

She burst into tears. Weird.

'Mam, don't worry about Sam and Gweena. I'll help you look after them. I'll help you with the cleaning as well.' The scraped chops tasted quite good.

She seemed to be really under the weather. She flopped into a chair near me and dabbed at her eyes. 'Gweena is competing tomorrow.'

'I know. It's brilliant.' Gweena is married to Sam, my dad's younger brother. I explained, 'That'll be the Cheese Inter-Hunt Chase. Her team must be through to the semi-finals.' Just the thing. Leg twitching with excitement. 'Mam, could I go to Punchestown? Please!'

'Yes, well I was planning to go there myself.' Again staring into space. She hadn't even mentioned that I'd miss school.

Maybe this was a good time ... 'Mam, I have to hunt Bluebell this year or I'll lose my place on the team. The chef d'equipe said I could join the Junior Hunt. It'll soon be starting up for the season. Trevor and Niall are joining and Paula will be hunting her new pony too. We could all go hunting together at mid-term. It might be held in Rathcoole, Newcastle, Castletown or Straffan. We could walk there.'

'Hmmm? Shhh. Don't shout. The hunt ... you're talking about experienced ponies, I'm sure. Yours is so green and so are ... well, you'd need supervision.'

'Mam, in the Junior Hunt they have supervision. They have the Green Coats riders who stay towards the back of the field and collect the stragglers.' Why did she think everything was dangerous? Better not to mention now what else Paula told me – that the Junior Hunt was invited to ride with the Ward Union Senior Hunt at Christmas ... with the hounds and all! She'd probably think I'd get trampled on and it would really put her off the idea.

I said quickly, 'There will be me and Trevor and Niall and Paula together. We can look out for each other.'

'We'll see.' She got up with an effort. 'Now, you said you'd help me ... '

'Yeah, well, Paula will be here any minute ... '

Still, I dusted the dressing-table and scrubbed the toilet and hand-basin in the en suite bedroom downstairs, then helped Mam make the bed. Every now and then she dabbed at her eyes. She is allergic to dust.

We hadn't got much homework for tonight. Only some Irish grammar. Easy.

'*Brisimid, Briseann sibh, Briseann siad* ... ' The approaching hoofbeats sounded different from Blackie's. Heavier. And faster. Already the big red horse was clomping past the window to the back door. Wow! I was standing there looking at him in amazement. He was some size!

Paula's voice floated down from a long way up. 'Tanoli is his name. Brilliant, isn't he?'

I stood there looking up at him. He had a kind of brainy look about him, all right. Sort of stiff, and snooty – his bug eyes showed no interest in me and were fixed on the roof of the house.

'His veins. They're popping out ... '

'Yeah. It's a sign of good breeding.'

'Yeah. And his knees. They're as big as soup bowls. He must be very strong. Like a war horse.' But not a very friendly one. 'I'd say he's had an amount of experience.'

The glass eyes were still unmoving. I thought, Bono and me are boring the life out of him.

Paula had leaned forward to stroke the big pony's neck. But he mustn't have liked that because all of a sudden he was rocking backwards and forwards on his legs like a giant rocking-horse and she had to grab at the reins to keep her balance. Bono stuck close to me until the rocking stopped.

Paula let out her breath. 'I thought he was going to rear.' Her eyes followed mine to his jagged tail. 'It's a switch tail,' she said, her voice cool again.

'Yeah, I thought so.' Better not say what I really thought – that something had eaten it. Or to ask her, 'Will you be jumping him?' The question just came out before I knew it.

She sat rigid between his ears and frowned. 'Not really. Polo ponies don't. It's like hockey on horseback and he's suffered stick injuries. Also, the chasing and stopping from full gallop in seconds and the sharp turns on hard ground damaged his tendons.'

'But, what about our hunt at mid-term?'

Paula stared at her pony's hogged mane. She said slowly, 'The vet did say he'd never be any use again. But Mrs M said that if he got plenty of roadwork his legs would harden and he'd be as good as any pony.' Her forehead cleared. 'Some ex-polo ponies have made good hunters. Good show-jumpers too.' She added in her determined way, 'I'll give him lots of roadwork to strengthen his legs. Yes, I'm sure he'll be able to hunt.'

My leg started hopping. Yes! We would go hunting at mid-term after all.

'He's a lovely horse.' Mam had joined us, recovered from her dust allergy, wiping floury hands on her jeans. She just had to butt in.

'Pony,' Paula corrected her politely.

The biggest pony *I'd* ever seen. He did not respond when I held out a hand for him to smell. Definitely not very friendly.

Paula's forehead was smooth again. She was speaking to Mam in her grown-up voice, 'He's an ex-polo pony. A full thoroughbred – well, nearly. Imported from Argentina.'

'Goodness.' Even though Mam seemed impressed she still made no attempt to pat him. Maybe because of that edgy look he was giving her.

'He's had many different owners and he's been with different ponies all the time. He's never had a chance to make friends or bond with anyone,' said Paula.

I could see Paula was right. He was not enthusiastic about us. This new pony was neither sociable nor trusting. Bluebell would miss her old friend after all.

Mam was walking around him, admiring him, still keeping her distance. 'What's his name?'

'Tanoli.'

'What a lovely name.' Then she added, 'Are you planning to play polo?'

'No.' Paula's forehead had crinkled again. She explained, 'His tendons failed and he was nearly sold for meat. A friend of my mother's rescued him and rested him up. He started jumping the fences and she knew she couldn't keep him. She didn't want him to go back to polo again so she sold him to us for a small fee.'

'That's wonderful ... ' Mam suddenly went rigid. 'Is that the phone ... ?' She almost tripped over Tanoli's big hoof in her hurry to get there.

'Don't bother answering, Mam.' I thought it was probably one of those phantom calls again. I heard her say 'Hello'.

Paula was interested in hearing about Punchestown and the Cheese Hunt Chase and I told her I was going there early to see Auntie Gweena and her hunter Strike.

Her voice was eager. 'Yeah, I could get a lift from my mum's friend and meet you there.'

She agreed that the Hunt Chase would give us an idea of what was in store for our ponies and us and what we should work towards before we went hunting. A loud snort came from the stable as Bluebell cleared her throat.

Tanoli's head turned and Paula suddenly burst out, 'Oh, my God. Do you see what he just did?'

'What?'

'He pricked his ears. He's interested in meeting Bluebell!' When she pulled on the rein the big pony twirled easily about and made straight for Bluebell's stable.

Bluebell strained over the door to get a look at him and when I led her out she smelled him inquisitively. But when she tried to rub noses with him he backed off and stared into the distance. She nuzzled my hand for comfort.

I said to Paula, 'Will we exercise in the field first?'

It was important to see how Bluebell and Tanoli got on together before taking them on the road – in case there was trouble. Paula gripped her reins tighter. She and Tanoli took off first and Bluebell was very interested, not taking her eyes off him. In trot, he covered a lot of ground and held his head very high.

'He's brilliant at neck reining.' Paula sat forward in a hunched position. Demonstrating like a cowgirl rounding up cattle, with only one hand on the reins, she twisted and turned him. Suddenly she pulled him up. 'God, I forgot! I nearly sprained his tendons again. I'll just canter him instead.'

This pony was big on performance. He hopped and skipped like a rabbit, then blasted off. He galloped at full speed, braked suddenly, then swung round and started again at full speed back towards us. Seconds before he was on top of us, he turned his long neck again. We stared after him. He was big, fast and spirited and very well sprung.

'See. He can go from canter to a stop in his own length. And he's great at doing flying changes – you know, changing leading leg in canter. I'll be able to do really difficult dressage tests. Eventually.' Paula looked down at us.

I told her I wanted to have a go on my pony.

'Okay – can I lead?'

Bluebell rushed after Tanoli. It wasn't easy following him because of his uneven canter and twice we nearly crashed into his tail when he braked. Then Bluebell made up her mind. She'd had enough. I could feel her disappointment. She had always been able to show off to Blackie. Show him her dainty heels. Before I could stop her, she whipped about and bolted with me back to the stable. She pretended to be drinking from the trough, plunging her muzzle deep into the water and splashing it out over the sides. I tried to get her to walk slowly back down the steep incline but she had other ideas. She broke into a gallop and swung right around, racing back up to the trough again. Eventually I took her down by the wall.

Whenever she misbehaved I turned her head towards it.

Paula rode over, smiling. She was on about her pony again. 'He'd be good in speed competitions but he's had enough for one day.'

'Okay. What about a game of chasing?' Bluebell was tensed up, all set for another race.

But Tanoli looked dignified and stared up at the sky. 'Can't.' Paula turned him for the gate. 'Will we go for a hack now before it gets too late?'

No jumping. But I knew Paula couldn't risk it. Tanoli could be damaged so easily. But that would all change, after he'd got plenty of roadwork.

We rode off together up the hill, Tanoli lengthening his stride and opening up a gap between us. I had plenty of space for thinking. Things had changed. This pony was serious and so was Paula. He was not for playing games or chasing about the field just for fun. He was not like Blackie. He was not just bigger, but faster and hotter. And reserved. He had his own thoughts and was not going to share them with Bluebell.

We trailed the big pony along the road. Paula was determined to strengthen his tendons and when he was back on track we could go hunting. I urged Bluebell to keep up.

Paula hardly spoke and looked grim, leaning forward in the saddle. Well, she would have a long way to fall. We took the lead. Bluebell trotted off in front but then there was a cry from Paula. Tanoli was rearing and misbehaving instead of following on.

'Would you mind letting me in front, thanks.'

Tanoli needed to go first. He liked it that way. Trouble was, Bluebell too wanted to lead. Tanoli's big walking strides outpaced her and in her disappointed mood she was in no form for trotting on, even when Tanoli went out of sight. Paula looked back now and then to see if I was coming and sometimes she waited for us. But even when we were together, having a conversation was not easy. My neck twisted and strained from looking up at her. Not being able to talk to her was the worst of all.

To be honest, I was glad when we turned for home. It was better once Bluebell speeded up.

Paula said firmly, 'For the next three weeks, roadwork only. Then Tanoli should be fit for jumping.'

No jumping for the moment. But roadwork and lots of it over the next few weeks. I could tell Paula was determined to stick to that fitness programme. Then we could go hunting together.

Before we parted we arranged where we'd meet each other next day at Punchestown before the start of the Hunt Chase.

Back home, Mam told me the phone call had been from Gweena. She and Sam would be very late arriving that night.

I tried to stay awake.

3 VISITORS

The window was all fogged up, icy to the fingers and outside it was misty too. Bluebell's head and neck stuck up like a ghost's above the swirling whiteness that covered the early morning grass. She nosed over the hedge at the lifeless jeep.

I slipped into the hallway and almost fell over a brown boot. As I hurried on to the kitchen, its faint sweet smell of dungy straw lingered with me.

'Well, Sarah, are you coming to see me in the Hunt Chase? We may not win today. The others on our team are no good.' Gweena sat on the worktop, her long legs sticking out from under her white night-shirt. She waved me over with the muesli packet. She is so tall that she usually sits on the table or a worktop or something, when there's no horse around.

I took the carton of dairy cream from the fridge. 'Is there a man in the green room?'

'That's Henry. He's our huntsman. Steady. Whoa.' She stopped me pouring. 'Anything you want to know about hunting, ask Henry. He was staying in the hotel with us but the manager asked him to leave when he didn't pay. I bought Strike, my horse, from him. Now, tell me about Bluebell. How is she going for you?'

'Fine. She's really cut out for cross-country. But she's not exactly in winning form.' I was trying to gobble my cornflakes, between wondering where Mam had left the special tea that Gweena likes and at the same time explaining to her what had happened last time out. She listened as if she were really interested.

'You can never tell what they are going to do when they go out. Anyway, she's young, isn't she?'

'Grandad says she's four.'

'Grandad.' Her finger poked disdainfully at the sliced pan. 'Henry will know.' She was so sure the man in the green room knew everything about horses. 'Yes, I suppose you'd better call him.'

The boots were gone and the room was empty.

'He's like a cat. He makes no noise when he's moving about.' Gweena took a sip of herbal tea and then a shadow passed the window. Gweena airily waved. 'That's Henry.'

A black-headed man in a shiny blue suit slipped in through the door and on to a chair beside me. That sweet smell. I love that smell. It reminds me of what horsy Heaven must be like. But my Mam hates it. And when she came in I thought she'd start opening windows and doors or looking for the Jeyes Fluid or talking about a clean and healthy environment or something. Instead, she hardly seemed to notice it – or Henry, for that matter. Which was surprising. And even when Gweena explained that Henry had slept in the green room, she just wandered off and got the frying-pan. Anyway, she's not really interested in horsy talk.

'That's a quiet pony you have. Where did you get her?' Henry spoke so softly you'd hardly know he'd said anything. I bet he could hear a horse talking. That special smell wafted from him, mixed with fry.

I said, 'Grandad got Bluebell for me for my birthday.'

Gweena interrupted me. 'What age do you reckon she is, Henry?' Her voice was full of respect.

'Five.'

Gweena looked satisfied, as if she had spoken to the Salmon of Knowledge. Anyway, I told them that Grandad had said Bluebell was 'four, rising five' – that was nearly the same thing. Gweena said nothing. Then, 'You'll be hunting her this year?'

I said quickly, 'Bluebell and me were never at a hunt.

But she'd be well fit for it. Our chef d'equipe says we should.'

'Your chef d'equipe is right, of course. Come to Galway. You can go hunting with me. It is good for a green pony to have an older experienced hunter with her. It would give Bluebell confidence. She'd be jumping big ditches without even noticing.'

I felt very happy at the thought and I echoed, 'She wouldn't even notice?'

'Yes. There's nothing like the sound of the horn and the hounds to excite them, even if it's a drag-hunt. Cross-country is very different. The horse is expected to jump cold. Hunting will definitely help, it will teach Bluebell to look after herself and that will give you confidence too. Just make sure your pony is fit.'

'Yeah.' It was exciting even hearing her talk about it. 'We're working on that at the moment. I've a friend who would like to come hunting too.'

I stopped. Mam was hovering over Gweena with the pan. 'Mam, I'm the only one who looked for sausages.'

'Hiya, Sarah. How's the pony?' Uncle Sam breezed in, hair slicked down, bath towels trailing. 'That was a great shower, Ann. I'll just dump these in the washing-machine. Henry, there's a shaver in the bathroom, if you want to give yourself a rub.'

My uncle is a horse trainer. Grandad always says 'the horses will break him'! But they haven't so far, not one bone, although I heard he had 'lots of hiccups'.

Outside, Bluebell whinnied over the hedge as I gave her some buttered and sugared bread and I told her, 'When I come back from Punchestown, I'll be getting after you.'

Gweena spoke sharply to me. 'Bad habit. She'll start nipping.'

Henry put his hand on her hind quarters. 'A quiet pony,' he murmured.

Gweena looked at her again and agreed. 'She has a nice kind eye.' She added to me, 'You'll have to turn that fat into muscle before you take her hunting.'

In the jeep, I shifted the bits of tack to sit on the muddy back seat beside Uncle Sam. Something hairy and warm was snuggling against the back of my legs. I looked down expecting to see a dog or a cat, only to find instead a little black and pink pig, fast asleep.

'Left turn for Desmond's,' Sam yelled.

Gweena swung in through the open iron gates, up a long avenue skirting the river, to a stone castle.

'Babe,' Sam called and stretched back his hands.

I scooped the little piebald pig off the floor and passed her out to Sam who carried her up the steps and pressed the bell. He handed over the pig; by now it was squealing its head off. The butler bowed to him and Sam got back into the jeep.

He explained: 'Strike's friend. One of the other horses tried to eat her. We'll get him a hairy goat instead.'

The early morning sun glittered on the flat dry grass in the car park where little tents were zipped tight against the sharp breeze. The smell of cooking drifted from lorries and trailers.

Sam, with bridle and Stübben saddle on his arm, strode ahead, ducking under ropes, and Gweena and Henry followed on with more horsy gear. I was hot on their heels, carrying Strike's grooming kit, which was fairly heavy. I was perspiring as we went through high gates into the stable yard. We wove our way through a row of hind legs. Wham! A nifty hoof grazed the grooming kit and knocked out the tin of saddle soap. Nothing serious and no one seems to notice as I bent down to return it. We hurried to the stable. There was the sound of pounding on the door.

Gweena shouted and it stopped. Strike pressed his big nostrils against the grille and blew. 'He doesn't like it here,' she said. She roared at him to get back from the door. But when Henry patted his forehead he relaxed and after that he was easy to manage.

I got a wheelbarrow for Sam and he borrowed the rake and poop-scoop and while he mucked out, I passed rubber bands to Gweena who had to stand up on the huge tack box to plait Strike's mane.

In the paddock I watched her exercise him and put him through his paces. He looked fit and muscular and his huge shadow followed him as he danced dangerously in the dust, black hooves crushing the earth. Gweena sat proudly in the saddle, her seat of honour.

'He's really brilliant,' I said to Henry. 'The way he sweeps over his fences.'

Henry barely shifted on the bale of straw. 'He rushes a bit.'

I said, 'I wish Bluebell could sweep over big fences like that.'

'You have a quiet pony.' That's all he said.

Later, in the Ladies, Gweena stood legs apart staring at

herself in the mirror. She looked fabulous, dressed in her green international riding-jacket, white skin-tight breeches and gleaming black leather boots. Like the model in an ad for *It* magazine. I helped to fix strands of her blonde hair under the hair-net and then she snapped her make-up bag shut. 'That's it.' She wanted to get back up on her horse, fast.

Strike was getting nervous from waiting around and Sam gave him a last polish with the stable rubber before Gweena mounted. I followed them to the show-ring where the teams were assembling for the parade.

On the way, I kept a watch out for Paula and my eyes wandered through the crowd. I saw a woman take a few steps towards a girl and hug her. In the distance, she looked very like Mam.

'Hi Sarah!' I turned to look in the other direction and there was Paula. She was red-faced from running. 'Mum's friend was delayed. I got a lift with Mrs M and Miranda.'

I took a deep breath, filling my lungs with crisp fresh air that no longer felt cold, only energising. 'You're wearing your jodhpurs ... I was grooming Strike all morning with Gweena. He's really spirited. He's a massive chestnut.'

Paula giggled. 'Can you imagine Tanoli here!'

'Yeah Bluebell and Tanoli!'

Paula gripped me my arm, pulling me along. 'Come on. We might get into the Riders' Pocket.'

Sounding his bugle, the pink-coated huntsmen led the members of the semi-final teams into the huge arena for the parade.

There, Strike was king, jostling the other horses and prancing on the spot, swinging his quarters in, swinging them out, doing half-passes, full passes. He was in a lather with excitement. When we shouted, Gweena shot us a quick smile, then steadied her horse again. Propped up in front of her on the saddle was the team mascot, a toy fox in a green riding-coat and breeches and long boots.

Paula and I discussed the course tactics for our ponies.

'Paula, you'll need to slow up on Tanoli going through a corral. You have to jump over the stile, turn quickly and jump out over the other stile ... '

'Yeah. But I guess we won't have these type of corrals out hunting.'

'It's not really very different from turning into a narrow laneway on a hunt, you know.'

'Isn't that a beautiful fly fence? The gate, I mean.'

'When Bluebell and me are faced with a gate out hunting, I'll just bend down and open it. My pony is steady. She allows me, she won't run away.'

'Yeah. Well, she might in a hunt when she's trying to keep up with other horses. But you'd want to motor on if you're going to take that water jump.'

'Oh God, would she be able for that?'

Paula said longingly, 'I wouldn't mind meeting a bank with water on the far side.'

'Bluebell wouldn't do that.'

'She will, if you drive her on. When she'll see the other horses doing it.' Then she nudged me and said fiercely, 'For goodness sake don't gallop off and leave me. Don't let your pony run off.'

I laughed happily. 'Bluebell mightn't jump at all.'

A fat man in a pink coat was riding for Gweena's team, the Galways. Paula, jumping up and down, described the action: 'He's overshot the corral, but he's through now.'

'What's happening, Paula?' I couldn't see very well. I jumped up on the seat. The riders from both teams were exchanging whips. Pink-coat was passing the whip to the long loopy one on a bony white horse. That must be old Bob. Hadn't a chance, Gweena said. His horse could drop dead any minute.

He trundled into the first fence. 'Oh, I can't see him ... ' A sudden cheer went up. His horse was back in view. He staggered on top of the huge bank but kept going. Then there was a groan and I saw a figure on the ground. Someone shouted, 'Yer man is down! Bob's ahead!'

Paula screamed, 'It's Gweena next. The Galways are in the lead. Come on, Gweena!'

Bob passed her the whip and she took off. Strike was completely uptight, foaming and snorting with nerves. But Gweena, standing in her stirrups, confidently checked him as they approached the first fence, steadied him, asked for his attention. From then on, he made the obstacles look like toys. He was a totally confident older horse, with loads of experience and daring. If Bluebell were behind him on the hunting field, nothing would stop her. Gweena rode like a champion and my leg lifted at each jump as they soared over. Strike gathered speed as he raced for the water jump. I lost sight of them.

'Aah ...' The crowd groaned and Paula gasped.

'Strike is running away with her!'

I saw him then. Something must have startled him. Instead of finishing the course, he was winding his head and galloping straight up through the arena, ignoring his fences. He turned at the bend, then came galloping in our direction. Gweena's foot was out of the stirrup and he was heading for the exit gate with her, thundering like a train. He was out of control.

Then, miracle! Henry appeared at the rails. I saw his black head move and saw Strike's ears go up, as if he had received a signal, and he checked himself. Gweena's foot was back in the stirrup and she was steering him towards the water jump.

They were out of sight. I waited for a splash but there was none, only a wild cheer. The Galways were into the finals.

'Strike is fantastic.'

'Yeah. But the obstacles aren't so bad. Tanoli could take them.'

I agreed. 'They're not so high.'

'Bob's horse is a bit like Bluebell.'

'Hmm. Well, Bluebell can really eat up the ground when she wants.' I was just about to tell Paula about Henry when she gripped my arm. 'Have you got a ticket?' The steward was coming towards us.

' Oh, God! No! Gweena forgot to give it to me.'

We ran for it and tried to squash into the grand stand.

'Can you see?'

'No. Not a thing. This is brutal.'

We raced from gate to gate, the cheers for the Galways cracking in our ears. 'Ahh. They've messed up the hand-over.'

At last we were able to squash in at the railings. Strike was backing away and rearing, not letting Bob's horse near him. Had they lost the chance? The whip was on the ground. We stopped shouting. The rival team had made the final handover and the rider was already half way around and carrying the whip over the finish.

We eased ourselves away from the railings. 'Strike got too excited.'

'Yeah. He thought it was a real hunt. But fair dinkum, he's a brilliant hunter!'

Paula led the way as we clambered over the emptying seats in a hurry to get down into the Riders' Pocket to meet Gweena and the other riders returning after the presentations. Then I saw Mam. She came out from the shadows at the back of the stand. She was wearing her new denim outfit. Who was she talking to?

'Paula, there's my mam.'

Paula stared. 'Isn't that Miranda with her?'

Maybe Mam was signing me up for Mrs M's Junior Hunt.

Mam was on her own when we reached her. Her hand was up to her eyes as if the sunlight was too bright. When she saw me she stepped towards me and flung her arms about me.

What was she on about? Gweena was beaten. Her team only got second ... And, anyway, win or lose, it wasn't like Mam to get that excited about any horse competition.

A horse brushed against her, separating us, and a red-cheeked Gweena slid out of the saddle. Grabbing Paula I pushed her forward to meet my aunt.

'Gweena', I said, 'this is my friend Paula ... '

But Gweena turned immediately to Mam and said loudly, 'See those blisters?' We studied the pink blotches on her fingers. 'That Bob, he wouldn't let go of the whip. He has the dead man's grip.'

Mam was nodding and smiling at her. Yet, I had the funny feeling that she hadn't heard a word Gweena was saying. And she was in the same weird mood driving home. The car was zooming past traffic, switching lanes. No matter what I asked her she said in a brimming voice, 'I don't know, dear. Ask Dad.' Then just before we pulled up at the house, she said excitedly, 'Sarah, I've something to tell you. Not now. Later.'

Must be to do with the Junior Hunt.

4 A SHOCK

'Dad, what's up with Mam? Is she going crackers or what?'

Dad had changed into his jeans and was pulling on his old grey jumper. 'We all have our problems.' He smoothed his bushy red hair. 'Now, you and I should have our tea.'

'What problems? What about Mam?'

With his arm about me he shepherded me into the kitchen. 'She has to drive over to Castleknock to see friends.'

'Castleknock? What friends does she have in Castleknock?'

He grabbed the kettle. 'I'll get the tea and you can watch *Neighbours*.'

'Can't I stay up for *The X-Files*?'

'We'll see.'

News time. War, floods, car crashes – where was Punchestown?

Then Mam opened the door wide. 'Sarah, I want to show you something. This is going to come as a big surprise.' Her voice and hand shook with excitement. As if what she held in her hands was the golden key that was about to open a treasure chest.

But all she had was a photo. I went over and looked at it. That face, those eyes, the big hair. I knew her. My heart began to thump.

'That's Miranda ... What's up? You're being completely scary.'

Mam took a deep breath. 'She's my daughter.'

'Your daughter? Is she my sister?'

Was this a joke? What was going on? I looked over at

32

Dad. But he was busy under the light at the sink, absorbed in trying to needle a thorn out of his finger.

Mam's voice was babbling on. 'She's your half-sister. We've been together today. I can hardly believe it after all the years of separation. It was pure chance that Miranda met you at Pony Camp and again at Mrs Montgomery's. An amazing coincidence. She thought you looked like her, Sarah, and that's how she found me.'

Miranda's ears stuck out like mine. That was all. She was prettier than me ... that strong, frizzy hair ... more like Mam's.

Mam was looking at the photo again, blinking hard.

'I called her Roisin, after my pet hen. Wasn't that silly?'

It *was* silly. I opened my mouth to tell her so, but my voice froze in my throat. Why was Mam behaving as if something wonderful had happened? She'd had this secret all these years. And she'd kept it from me ... and Dad. Did Dad know?

At last: 'You should have told me.'

'I didn't know where she was until today. She found me. It's a miracle.'

I repeated, 'You should have told me.'

She opened her arms. Above my head her voice floated out of darkness. 'Sarah, I know you and Miranda will get on very well. And I'll need your help because I'll have to get to know the child I lost all these years ago.'

I pushed her away, then mumbled about being tired, needing to go to bed.

Already Mam was making plans for me to get to know Miranda. She said it was great that we were both interested in horses. That Miranda would be coming to stay at our house for weekends just as soon as it could be arranged with her other parents. They were very nice people. Miranda would not like to hurt them.

This was a disaster and Mam was making it sound like a picnic. I slipped back to my room where I could think. Maybe everything would be better in the morning.

I heard Dad's voice: '... a shock ... you must give her time .... Things are happening too fast, too soon. Why don't you ring the social worker. Get some advice ... '

'I'm her mother. We've been separated too long. I don't want anyone delaying things further. We're going to deal with it our own way.'

The voices faded. And then I'm dreaming of Bluebell in the lead, chasing through the fields, taking the stone walls and hedges and ditches in her stride, Paula flying along on Tanoli, Strike's huge dark bulk galloping dangerously close and all the other horses pounding behind us.

And then I'm opening a gate. But a big dark hand reaches up out of the muck and catches my boot. It's trying to pull me off my pony. I'm screaming but no one can hear me. Bluebell is stretching like elastic. I'm trying to kick free of the hand. The fingers are mashed and bloody but won't let go and even when I kick them off they grow again, long and bony with black nails and white pus oozing from under them. I'm slipping off, going down, down. I'm going to be trampled to death...

Someone was moaning. I woke up and it was very dark.

Then I heard a sound and I no longer felt panic. Blue-bell's whinny was soft.

I thought of something new. Miranda. My sister! Would I ever be able to say that word out loud?

Past the paddock, everything was hidden behind a grey mist. There was a ball of dread in my stomach. I tried to swallow the hard bit of toast.

'Where's Dad?'

'He's ... ' She hesitated. I knew she wanted to talk about Miranda.

I got up. 'We'd better hurry. I'll be late.'

Mam's window wipers swished excitedly at the coating of mist. I caught a few words. ' ... so much lost time to make up with Miranda.' Had Mam been talking to herself or to me? I hoped Paula was in early.

The grey rain was drizzling down and forming puddles in the playground. There was no sign of Paula. With this weather, we'd be stuck in the classroom all day, not even getting out at break-time, which meant that I probably wouldn't see her for the whole school day. And I badly needed to talk to her.

'Hey, wait up!' Niall hurried after me down the corridor. 'Got the teabags for Teabag?'

'Oh, no. I forgot.'

'His eyes are still gooey.' He paused near my desk, shuffling the wet out of his hair. 'Bluebell okay?'

'Fine.'

'Are you going out riding after school?' As I nodded he added, 'We might join you.' He was captain this week and it was his job to collect the copybooks. Nicole, Trevor's latest, was leaning to one side, showing him her answers. He was smoothing his long sleeked-back hair and securing it with a rubber band. I heard him ask, 'How do you spell cathedral?'

I wished it were break-time. The Irish lesson went slowly. We were describing *an chlann*. The family. Teacher was asking Trevor about his. Two? I whispered to Niall that I thought that there were four in his family.

'Were,' he corrected. 'He's living with his dad now. His sister is with his mother.'

Then suddenly the teacher was asking me how many in mine.

This was embarrassing. Miranda was not really my sister. She didn't live with us. What was I going to say? The class was staring at me, waiting. *'Ta triur sa chlann.'* Or were there four in my family. I didn't know any more.

Babs was sniggering from the front seat. 'She doesn't know how many in her family.'

'Triúr sa chlann.' Mrs Pyne repeated it firmly and moved on. She was asking Babs about her own family. Who was the eldest- luckily she hadn't asked me that one.

'Mise...' Then Babs spluttered. *'Ni hea ... Seán ... '*

Mrs Pyne raised her eyebrows. 'You're not so smart when it comes to your own turn, Babs. You'd better write

up the lesson and hand it in tomorrow.'

Babs made a face behind her back.

Wait until she found out about Miranda. She'd wonder why I said three and not four. I looked down at the open page of my copybook and realised I'd scribbled all over it. Miranda... Miranda... Miranda... I quickly used the rubber.

In the playground, Babs was racing about me. Saying things to me. About Katie, I think. Pressing her big face close to mine. ' ... Did you hear what I said?'

'What? No. Sorry. There's Paula.'

I ran to the school door to meet her as she came out.

Paula's forehead was in a knot. 'Why did your mother give Miranda away?'

'I don't know.'

'I would never make that mistake. Having a baby, I mean, and then giving it away,' Paula said thoughtfully. 'Where is she now?'

'She was adopted. By a family living in Castleknock. At least I think so. Mam went to see them. I think that's where she is now.'

Paula said, 'I don't think it's fair to bring Miranda back into your lives. She has her own parents.'

The bell rang and we had to get back into line. But I felt better. The day was brighter and the rain had stopped. We could hack out on our ponies after all.

Bluebell whinnied as soon as I got off the bus. She pushed her soft muzzle over the hedge and I blew into her nostrils. She quivered with pleasure. 'I'll be with you in a minute,' running up the driveway. She ran alongside me on the far side of the hedge.

I said to Paula, 'I mean, Miranda doesn't even like me.'

'But she doesn't really know you – yet.' She jumped up and swept her riding-hat off the bed, telling me to hurry up. 'We've work to do.'

I'd forgotten all about heating up my dinner, now that Mam wasn't around to do it.

Paula switched on the cooker. 'Make it fast. You know it gets dark early.'

'Niall wanted to hack out with us. His pony needs to get fit too for hunting this season.'

Paula led the way. 'Hasn't Teabag got conjunctivitis?'

'No. It's just an autumn cold.'

But Paula wouldn't wait for Niall. She said his pony would cause too much excitement and this would be bad for Tanoli. She was moving ahead, looking critically back at Bluebell.

'Yeah, Bluebell is now much better co-ordinated and the experience she'll get from hunting should bring her on even more,' I said.

'Yeah, I suppose so.'

I was happy enough to let Bluebell lag behind Tanoli. Picturing what she and I would be doing soon. Very soon...

She's chasing through big stubble fields with the other hunters, taking the big banks and fallen trees and fences in her stride. Racing through forests, leaping over stone walls and ditches. What I see is not a show ground or an artificially confined course. What I see is big country where her herd instinct can run free. With a freedom of the plain and hill and mountain. Of forest and meadow. Of old lanes and bridle paths. I can picture us crossing gushing streams and wide rivers. And I can see Grandad in the distance following in the jeep, Suki his dog sitting beside him in the passenger seat...

'That's no way to build your pony's muscles. Can you not ride on?' Paula's sharp voice prodded me out of my dreams. I rode on, still full of future plans.

My plans did not include Miranda.

5 MIRANDA'S VISIT

After the rain, chickweed spread over the potato patch and into the paddock among the docks and nettles. The grass was sleek and glowing as if lit from down under. Yellow-bellied slugs clustered in old feeding saucepans, still searching for a juicy feed. Hidden briars lurked under the scutch grass and their strong tendrils stretched out to trip up animals and humans alike.

I took a very deep breath. 'I've got a half-sister. She's adopted.'

'Oh yeah?' Niall kept on writing up last night's homework. He didn't seem awfully interested but when I told him it was Miranda, he gave a low whistle. Immediately I wished I hadn't. He said loudly, 'Miranda at Mrs M's? She's all right.'

Trevor was passing and he clattered him on the head with his maths book. 'Miranda – what about Miranda?'

Niall rubbed his head. 'Easy man! She's Sarah's sister.'

My sister. My teeth clenched to hear him say it. But Trevor was looking at me with new interest. As he and Niall sat down I heard him say, 'Yeah, she's amazing.' And he wasn't talking about me. I could see the curious look on Babs's face as she whispered something to Katie.

We'd been given a half-day for the teachers' meeting. Babs asked me to walk with her up the hill, waving Katie off in her parents' car, refusing their lift. 'I hate Katie. She's so boring. She thinks she's my best friend. I can't get rid of her.' She was in a very good mood. Even offered me a polo mint. Her last one ... well, second-last ...

'Miranda is your sister, is she? Must be awful. I'd hate to have an older sister, bossing me an' all.' She clucked sympathetically, jumped up on the ditch then pretended to topple out in front of a car. The driver shook his fist at us.

'Thanks.' I explained about Miranda and I could see Babs was listening very carefully by the way she narrowed her eyes. She clucked again and it seemed she was feeling very sad for me. I told her, 'Miranda should have stayed away. She was in the past. Dad and Mam and me are the present. She has her own set of parents now.'

Babs said gloomily, 'Your parents probably prefer her to you. Like, she's the eldest now.'

'Yeah. The eldest grandchild too.'

'Yeah. The eldest grandchild is always special. Mostly gets the presents.'

'Yeah. I used be the eldest. And my grandad's favourite.' Maybe that could change too, even though Miranda wasn't really *his* grandchild.

'Yeah. Probably take away all your friends. She's so good-looking an' all. Niall and Trevor were talking about her. They couldn't shut up about her.' She said in a sad voice, 'You have a big problem.' She was very attentive, patting me on the head in sympathy, squeezing my arm and pinching me on the cheek. She was being very nice to me and I needed it.

'Yeah. Thanks, Babs.'

'Yeah. If that was me, I'd run away.'

I stopped up. The mention of running away had opened up a very sore memory in my brain. The disappearance of Bluebell and Babs's part in it. 'Yeah, well – I'll wait and see if things get any worse.'

We said good-bye at the gate.

'Will you be coming up after, Sarah?'

'I have to go out on my pony. Bye, Babs.'

'Byee.' She grinned happily and when Bono licked her through the gate her grin spread wider and she skipped up the road.

I threw down my school-bag. 'Mam, what are you doing? What's that smell?'

'Miranda is a vegetarian. She's coming for dinner this evening. I looked in last night to tell you when I got home but you were asleep. You'll be here when she comes, won't you?' Another saucepan clattered on to the worktop to join the other pots and pans and there was a thump as it dislodged one of the cookery-books. Red-faced, Mam ignored it, and whipped open another.

I picked up the *Encyclopaedia of Creative Cooking* off the floor and replaced it. 'You know I can't, Mam. You know Paula and me have a busy training schedule every evening. I can't change that. Do you want me to spoil my pony? Do you? Wreck my team's chances of winning?'

'You've nothing coming up immediately. Anyway, Miranda could help you with the training. And with Tanoli's too.'

'What does she know about my pony? She hasn't got her A-Test yet.'

'She'll soon have her B-Test. She's preparing for that now, as you know. Her Horsemastership.'

'Mam, I have my D-Test, remember?'

'Yes, of course, dear. But she's had a lot of experience working in yards, riding different horses ... '

Mam was very knowledgeable all of a sudden.

'She's not that experienced. She's never had a pony of her own. Only "school" ponies.'

Mam sounded pained. 'Please. I'd like you to be nice to her.'

'Well, okay. I'll wait.' I rang Paula to tell her.

'Your mother is right. This is a chance for you to get to know each other,' Paula said. 'We can exercise in the field and hack out later – if that's okay with your dad.'

I helped to chop up the vegetables for the soup – carrots, potatoes, onions, turnips and celery. A whole garden going into it. My hand was tired from peeling. I wouldn't be able to hold the reins after this. Mam didn't care. She had

made a pot of rice for Miranda. Now it was a lentil stew –
she checked the label on the margarine: 'Animal fat ...
can't use that ... ' flinging it aside, grabbing for the olive oil
instead. Ticking off ingredients, '... ginger, spuds, paprika
– what else? Oh no! I forgot to soak the beans!' Lentils:
dark green ones, brown ones, big ones, little ones ... grains
of barley ...'

'Have to go, Mam. Paula is here.' I was glad to escape. I
definitely wouldn't be around for the washing-up.

For ten minutes we concentrated on limbering up, riding
in figures of eight, circles, serpentines and loops to get our
ponies to bend their broad backs and their whole bodies,
to increase their suppleness and tone their muscles. Then
Bono barked loudly from the gate – Miranda had arrived.

'It's family time. Good luck. See you later.' Paula waved
to Miranda in the distance before riding off. I could see
Miranda waiting for me up at the stable so I tried to delay
by completing a few more circles but Bluebell wasn't in the
humour now that Tanoli was gone. She bolted with me to
the stable and I pretended that was what I wanted to do all
the time. 'Hi! there ... Bluebell is sweating ...'

'But she looks happy.' She certainly looked happy now
with Miranda patting her face, speaking gently to her.
'Lady, you do what you like, don't you?' and Bluebell just
nudged her playfully.

I spoke in a no-nonsense voice to her: 'Don't do that,
Bluebell. It's not funny.' But I really felt annoyed. Bluebell
should not be acting so friendly. After all, Miranda was a
stranger, almost.

I changed the conversation a bit. 'What do you think of
Paula's new pony. He's brilliant, isn't he?'

'Hmm. Paula could help him more. She's very stiff.'

'She has to ride like that,' I said quickly. 'She's afraid
he's going to rear.'

'He wouldn't if she wasn't so tense.' Miranda coolly
blew into Bluebell's nostrils and Bluebell gave a whinny of
a laugh.

Were we going to stand here all day? I said, 'I suppose we'd better go in.'

At the back door I waited but she said, 'After you,' and for once she didn't seem so certain of herself, as if she thought she might be at the wrong house. How I wished she were.

Mam mustn't have heard us come in with the hum of the fan oven. Her back was to us.

Miranda spoke. 'Ann – Mom.'

I barely heard Mam's quick gasp or saw her face light up.

It was as if I had got a heavy fall off Bluebell; I was hardly able to breathe from the shock of hearing her call *my* mother 'Mom'. My mother was her mother too. I was left gasping for breath for ages – all the time they were hugging each other.

At last Mam said in a muffled voice, 'Sarah, go and tell Dad that your big sister is here.'

A sister I never knew existed. I felt an arm around me and it was Dad. He was smiling too. Standing by to welcome her. And after he'd given her a big shake-hands and put her sitting down in his own chair – the one with the straight back on it- he chatted to her until Mam asked me to get her a drink of coke. At that he shot off to get it for her himself.

Miranda turned to me smiling, real friendly-like. Her mounds of purple eye-shadow had smudged. I listened with my mouth open as she gabbled on and on about how lucky we were to be living in the country. She'd thought she recognised me at Pony Camp that first day, only she didn't like to say anything because she had often thought someone looked like a brother or sister and she was afraid of making another mistake ... Was this the same Miranda who hardly spoke to me before?

Mam took down the photo-album from the shelf and left it on the worktop. She smiled shakily. 'I must show you some photos after dinner ... we'll have lots of time to talk.'

She bustled about, then suddenly put her hand on my shoulder. It was getting really boring. And where was Dad with the coke? I could do with a drink as well. Mam was asking me to show my sister around.

I brought Miranda just to the door of my bedroom. But she strolled in and started looking at my pony library. She was asking if she could borrow one of my pony magazines, the special supplement on the 25 secrets of the real Horse Whisperer. She patted a space beside her on my bed. 'I want to show you something.'

I sat down and waited while she took some photographs from a wallet.

'These are my parents, the ones I live with. And that's my older brother. He's adopted too. He was a great help. He was able to get some information for me in a round-about way that confirmed things about my mom. After that, the jigsaw fitted.'

She was showing me another photo, this time of herself with a boy wearing earrings. He had a ring in his forehead. Probably had his tongue pierced too. 'That's Yaqoub, my boyfriend. He goes to my school. His father is an Arab.'

'Have you ever met his father?'

'No. He lives in Tangiers.'

Maybe she'd go there. For good. She explained, 'Yaqoub lives with his mother. She's very nice.'

'What about your parents? Do they like him?'

Miranda shrugged. 'It's none of their business … want a piece?'

'Thanks.' I took the chewing-gum. I wasn't going to, but I couldn't refuse, seeing as it was my favourite flavour, mint. We chewed together in silence. Then I said, 'Was it you who made those phone calls to Mam?'

'Yes.' She said slowly, 'I wanted to hear her voice.'

'Why didn't you speak to her when she answered?'

'I was afraid she wouldn't want me. I lost my nerve.' She was staring hard at the empty gum wrapper in her hand. This was more like the Miranda I knew. Moody. Strangely,

it made me feel happier. I didn't have to like this Miranda.

'The people who adopted you ... are they not good to you?' Why had she bothered to find my mam and cause all this disturbance?

'Oh, yes, they are. They're really good to me.' She paused. 'But I just wanted to find my real mother. See what she looked like ... where I got my hair, my eyes, my ears ... my interest in horses and in art ...' She gave a short laugh. 'Now I have two families. And everyone wants me to come and live with them, starting this weekend.'

My gum made a loud pop as it burst. 'But that was in the past. We're strangers.'

'Yes. But we can get to know each other, can't we?'

Just then Mam rushed in to tell us that dinner was ready. Going out of the room she put an arm around each of us and hugged us to her. 'This is the happiest day of my life.'

'Mam, you're squeezing me.' I shrugged myself free. How could my mother say this was the happiest day of her life? What about me? Mam told me to put the gum away.

I was trying to eat my way through a heap of weeds.
Dad's tongue was hanging out for a piece of meat and it
was all green, like Bluebell's. The conversation wasn't
helping. Only for that I might have been able to pretend I
was Bluebell and swallow some of it, just to be polite. But I
was too afraid that I'd choke on it.

Dad said, 'So you're doing your B-Test. Fair play to
you.'

'Yes. I can teach the little ones at Pony Camp. Earn
some money during the holidays. Helps pay for my riding-
lessons.'

There was silence. Dad shuffled his beans and Mam said
quickly, 'Miranda, if you're short of money ... '

'No, no.'

I felt a lentil stick in my throat and hoped I wouldn't
choke on it. Mam never asked me if I was short of money.

Dad's tongue was back in his mouth. He threw down his
knife and fork and said in a sad voice, 'Horses are a lovely
pastime.'

'Yes.' Miranda turned to me. 'What about you, Sarah?
You did your D-Test at Pony Camp, didn't you?'

'Yeah. I'm going to do my C-Test next year if I can. '

'I could help you with that.'

'Thanks. But Paula has a lot of practical experience.
We'll work on it together.'

Mam said anxiously, 'You're not eating, Miranda. I'm
afraid the vegetables got a little overdone ... '

Burned was the word she was looking for.

'They're lovely. I'm just not very hungry.'

'Maybe at the weekend ... '

I'd had enough. I stood up. 'I have to go now. I told
Paula I'd hack out with her and it will be getting dark
soon.'

Miranda got up too. 'I've got a present for you here, somewhere.' She tossed the long soft parcel in my direction and
was gone out to the stable.

Mam, gathering up the dishes, said dreamily, 'She's so kind and generous – as you are too, Sarah. It's wonderful to see you getting on so well together. Now, let's see what she brought you.'

It was a white sheepskin numnah. This certainly would prevent Bluebell's saddle chafing her. Just what she needed. Suddenly I wanted to be out there in the stable with Miranda and Bluebell and I jumped up from the table. 'I'd better put it on my pony right away.'

Why didn't Bluebell whinny at my approach? I soon saw why. Miranda was totally distracting her. She was feeding Bluebell from a small packet with what looked like balls of mud. I said sharply, 'Don't give her those.'

'They're herbals. Haven't you seen them before?' Miranda explained and went on feeding her and I heard her murmur, 'A special treat for the cutest pony.'

'She won't like them,' I said.

And then I had to stand there and watch Bluebell guzzling.

'They're all gone, Bluebell.'

But Bluebell kept nosing at the crinkling packet in Miranda's pocket and drooling. It wasn't fair. She was treating Miranda like an old friend. And Miranda was encouraging it. After all, Bluebell was *my* pony.

'Do you want to try on the numnah? Here, give it to me.'

She helped to me put it on under the saddle.

'It really suits her.' I couldn't keep the pride out of my voice at the sight of my pony wearing her new numnah. Miranda was saying nothing. I waited, expecting to hear her say my pony was beautiful. She was stroking Bluebell between the eyes giving her a sorrowful air.

'Where did Bluebell come from?' When she did speak her voice was casual.

'My grandad in Galway got her for me. I think she lived on a mountain.'

'You know who your parents are.'

Was she talking to Bluebell? She turned her face to me. 'Do you know her pedigree? Her dam and sire?'

'Not really. Grandad didn't say.' Well, it wasn't that important, was it?

She still sounded calm. Her hand stroked Bluebell, never leaving my pony's forehead. 'I would have loved a pony of my own and to live here in the country ... with my real family.'

'Yeah, well ... ' I could see she liked my pony, all right. Now Bluebell was lathering her hand with her tongue and Bono was trying to get in on the act too. I booted him away. Wait until he tasted the heap of rotten leftovers in his dish – not even a rasher rind – and he wouldn't be so happy with Miranda then.

I told her, 'I'll be late. I'd better go. You'll probably be gone by the time I get back.'

She gave Bluebell a last pat. 'Probably ... but I may be here again tomorrow.'

Paula leaned out of the saddle to feel Bluebell's new numnah. The brand name 'Redwings' was tops.

I wailed, 'You should have seen the dinner Mam prepared. She never went to that kind of trouble for me. It took her hours. Lentils and stuff. It was yucky. And she didn't care if we liked it or not so long as Miranda did. Disgusting.'

I didn't tell Paula about Mam saying it was the happiest day of her life. Even thinking about it gave me a pain in my side, as if someone had stabbed me.

Paula straightened in the saddle. 'Will she be coming to live with you?'

Someone was twisting the knife. 'I don't know. I think Mam wants her to come and stay this weekend.'

'What are you going to do?'

'Probably stay in my room all the time if I have to.'

But I didn't have to.

6 GOING TO GRANDAD'S

Next day, I told Paula about the new development.

'There's a show on in Galway this weekend,' I explained, 'and Grandad wants me to be there. Dad thinks it's a good idea, that Bluebell could do with the outing.'

'How will you get to it?'

'Dunno. I asked Dad about a horse-box but he just told me not to worry. It's on Saturday so we'll probably have to leave early on Friday.'

Paula looked away. I knew what she was thinking. She'd have to hack out on her own while I was away.

I said suddenly, 'Maybe you could come too. We might even be able to borrow a double horse-box – then you could bring Tanoli.'

But Paula shook her head. 'Mum is busy at work. She needs me around.' She burst out, 'I wish my dad hadn't died – then he could be arranging things like that for me.'

'Yeah. My dad is good all right.' At least he wasn't going out of his head fussing about Miranda.

There was a shout. 'Good throw!'

'You've landed it in the graveyard – you're stalling.'

'I'm not! Sarah bumped into me.'

'Sorry!' We quickly moved off the basketball area where we had strayed. I explained to Paula, 'Grandad thinks Bluebell will be fit for the showing class. He's the chairman of the committee and all and he wants us to compete so that he can show off me – I'm his favourite grandchild – and Bluebell to his friends. I probably won't be in to school on Monday either.'

Paula said, 'Be sure you're back on Tuesday then.' She

49

added thoughtfully, 'What about Miranda? Won't she miss you if you're not around for the weekend?'

I stared at Paula. She sounded as if she were worried about Miranda. But she'd got it all wrong. I said, 'She'll have Mam all to herself.'

'It'll be nice to have Miranda here.' Why did Mam have to look so happy at the thought? 'Pity you can't leave Bluebell behind. She'd be well looked after while you're gone.'

It wasn't enough to have Mam all to herself for the weekend. She needed my pony too.

I said, 'I don't think so.' Mam was trying to get rid of me and keep Bluebell for Miranda. But Bluebell and me were not going to be separated. No way.

The knife in my hand left a little gash in the oilcloth. 'I have to take her. She's entered. Grandad would lose the entry fee if she didn't go in the competition.' I tried to keep my voice happy, not to let Mam hear the sulk in it. 'Anyway, Grandad is proud of me. He wants his grand-daughter's pony to compete.'

Mam didn't seem to notice my bad mood. She ventured, 'Did you have any luck yet with ... '

The knife clattered on the table. 'Mam, you keep asking me that. We'll find a horse-box. You needn't worry.'

I was shouting. Mam looked shocked but I didn't care.

There was a tap at the window. Dad's face was squashed up against it and he was beckoning at us to come outside.

Something was parked behind his car.

'What is it?' Mam sounded doubtful.

'What do you think it is?' He looked at it proudly.

I asked, 'Is it a bread van?'

It was a peculiar shape, heavy and angular. On the timbered sides you could just make out the faded words 'Ann's Hot Bread' printed under the lime-green paint.

''Was,' Dad corrected. 'Now it's a damn fine horse-box.' He patted its steel frame. 'Fit to carry a fine pony to Galway.'

'Thanks, Dad.' I hugged him. At least my Dad still wanted me. Me and him and Bluebell would be happy enough. 'Dad, do you think it will it fit under the railway bridge?'

He didn't hear me. He was trying to unhitch it from his car but he couldn't get it off. He straightened, red-faced. After wiping his forehead he patted the trailer again. 'It's a good strong heavy one.'

Mam said, 'You'll need a hand with that. You could strain yourself.'

'There's no need ...'

But she had gone off to ring Miranda.

I hugged Dad again. Bluebell could travel with us. Yippee! It would be her first really long journey in ages – in a horse-box. And there would be just the three of us.

Paula let Tanoli smell the box. She reckoned it might take two ponies to the hunt when we were ready.

'You can't take Bluebell on that journey without a travelling rug and travelling boots. Miranda could probably borrow them for you from Mrs M.'

Well, I wasn't going to ask her. I phoned Niall.

Niall was at the school gate, waiting. He helped me to stuff the boots into my bag. These boots would go right up her legs and protect them in case Dad braked suddenly or cornered sharply and she fell over or scrambled about and cut herself.

'What about the rug?'

'If she wasn't wearing one, she doesn't need one now. She'd only sweat up.'

'Yeah. Guess you're right. Thanks.' We joined the crush going into the computer room.

I wanted to stay with Bluebell in the horse-box for the journey, but Dad wouldn't hear of it.

We set about loading her. I bandaged her tail and then I put on the travelling boots and her head-collar complete

with the poll guard Paula had lent me in case she reared and hit her head off the roof. Next, we had to load her. Dad opened the side door so that there was plenty of light in the box.

I led her to the ramp but she refused to put a hoof up on it. So Dad and Paula linked hands and shoved her up. Once inside, standing on straw, she munched in comfort at the fresh hay in the net.

I raced over to Mam and kissed her good-bye. Miranda hadn't arrived yet. Starting off down the hill, Dad remarked, 'I thought the box might be too heavy for the car. But we seem to be going very well.'

We travelled smoothly until we came to the hump-backed bridge over the canal. The car and trailer crawled over the top and Dad let out his breath as we trundled down. 'It's a very heavy box, all right.'

Passing through Celbridge, Bluebell called loudly. In town after town and village she announced herself and the windows in the houses rattled with the shrill delighted whinny, as if she knew she was heading in the direction of her old home.

Flying down the hill into Tyrrellspass we got a speed wobble and we swayed from side to side with Bluebell zig-zagging behind us. It was scary! But somehow Dad managed to straighten it out and we travelled fairly smoothly after that.

There was something I wanted to ask him. I took a deep breath. 'Dad, why did Mam give Miranda away?'

'She wasn't able to mind her. She was only seventeen years old and on her own. Her parents couldn't take care of her because one of them – her father – was seriously ill at the time.'

'But what about the ...father?'

'He was young too. He didn't want to know. He went to Canada.'

I dozed off. Then a white-hot thought flashed across my brain, jerking me wide-awake. Mam gave Miranda away. Maybe she had wanted to give me away too but Dad wouldn't let her.

'After Mam gave her away, why didn't she try to contact her? Did she not want her back or what?'

'We had no way of knowing where she was. We had decided that we would try to contact her again when she was eighteen years old – at that age she could start searching. It was a shock when she turned up out of the blue. We had no idea where she was.'

'Dad, do you think she'll be coming to live with us?'

'I'd have my doubts that it would be possible ... Now,' around the next bend of the road, 'we're here.'

Granny and Grandad's house was lit up and Grandad's hatted figure stood waiting in the doorway. We pulled up but he made no move. I called out to him and at the sound of my voice he came hurrying out on to the road.

His mouth was open in surprise. 'I didn't recognise ye

with the van. I thought it was Paddy Joe Whatchamacallim
– he had a van like that when he was tarrin' the road for
the council years ago.'

'It's a horse-box, Grandad.' A kiss and a hug for him.

'Hmm.' He was smiling now. 'It's a fine heavy box. And
that's a great car to pull it – as good as a tractor. I thought
ye'd never get here. Right, Shane. Take her down. Don't
mind the cars. They can take their time – speedin' goin'
mad, reckless.' He was impatient, waving his torch at the
oncoming cars so that they had to stop and dim their
lights.

Bluebell whinnied softly as she came down the ramp and
Grandad took hold of her head-collar and led her on to the
footpath. His voice sounded amazed. 'What happened her?
She's all covered up.' He peered closer. 'She's after turnin'
into a fine little mare. And she knows where she is too –
see how she's lookin' around her. They say a horse has a
great memory and there's no doubt about it. Nature is a
wonderful thing.'

Giving her to me to hold, he called out to Dad, 'You'd
better not park the box there … some lunatic would only
crash into it and kill himself – and sue you into the
bargain.' Muttering something about insurance claims, he
directed Dad up the boreen to park.

Keeping to the footpath, we walked Bluebell up to the
orchard field chosen by Grandad for her and led her
through the big gate. It was dry and shady here.

He had prepared the calf shed for her. A thick bed of
oaten straw covered the floor. First, we let her graze for
half an hour on the head-collar. Grandad said, 'She loves
the fresh grass and herbs.' Then he carried a section of a
bale of hay to the water tank and submerged it. 'The dust
would only give her a cough,' he wheezed. 'Turn off that
light. It has me blinded.'

I watched her sniff about the shed, nuzzle at the hay and
straw. Grandad brought her a fist of oats in a bucket and
she began to eat. We watched for a few more minutes to

make sure she had settled. Then he said we should go for
our tea.

'Next time we're here,' I said, 'me and Bluebell might be
able to go hunting.'

The old knife he used for cutting the baling twine
tinkled into the crevice in the wall where he kept it.
'Huntin'! Keep well away from it!'

'But, Grandad, Paula wants to go hunting too. Gweena
said she'd take us.'

'Stick to yer little shows where ye'll be safe. That's my
advice.' He held up a huge padlock. 'Now, switch off that
flash-lamp. It's destroyin' the light. Ah, that's better. Now
I can see what I'm at.'

He locked the gate after us and dropped the key into his
waistcoat pocket. Grandad was not a man to take chances.
'You wouldn't know who'd take a fancy to that little pony.'

There wasn't much work in preparing her for the show – I
washed the mane and tail as Grandad advised and he
trimmed the end, no need to plait. I'd oiled the hooves and
Grandad had oiled around her muzzle. He had another
showing secret too; he cut a little square of mane at the
poll where the bridle rests. The bridle was an old one with
brass fittings, which he had resurrected for Bluebell.

Getting to the showgrounds was no trouble either with
our new horse-box. And Bluebell, being well used to
shows, behaved in a calm and well-controlled manner and
when the assistant had waved his catalogue as a signal to
us, she had cutely walked around in a circle with the other
ponies. It was exciting when she was waved in first to do
her individual showing.

Grandad had positioned himself where she'd walk to the
ropes, clapping his coat to make her walk towards the
judge, signalling me to give her a tip behind with the lead
rein and get her to look lively. Leaning over the rope,
almost capsizing: 'Don't drag her after you. Make her walk
up smartly beside you.' He had shown me how to hold it

up short and long at the other end.

I was a little bit disappointed when she'd been put back to second place. I'd had to trot her up and down and she hadn't trotted out. Grandad said she must have eaten some of her nice straw bed and that had left her a bit sluggish.

'Your mother was on the phone twice,' said Granny. 'She wants you to ring back.'

'Tell Dad.'

'He won't be back for hours once he gets to meet the old cronies!'

'I'll do it later.'

'Do it now, then go to bed.'

'Later, Granny. Grandad wants me to watch television with him.'

He snored for a while, then shuddered and woke up. 'Where was I? ... Er, what about Miranda?'

So *he* knew about Miranda too. More secrets.

'She's staying the weekend with Mam. She wants a pony too.' The ads were on.

Grandad seemed to think about it. 'If I got her a pony like Bluebell she'd probably say there was somethin' wrong with her, that she had a wall-eye or somethin' else.'

'Grandad, Bluebell has a wall-eye.' But I knew what he meant. Miranda would be hard to please.

'Anyway, ye couldn't keep any more than one pony up in your place. Where would ye put it?'

For some reason, I was glad to hear that. I waited but he had gone to sleep again.

Granny was at the door again, this time with my hot-water bottle.

Lying in bed I thought of Bluebell alone in the little stone-walled field. It was her first trip back to Galway since she had left it as a filly. Maybe Grandad would take me to visit the mountain where she came from.

And Mam. Well, Mam had Miranda.

7 CRISIS

Cobwebs sagged with dewdrops in the box hedge which divided the lifeless vegetable garden from the orchard. The branches of the apple trees stuck up like old dark bones against the frosty sky. Near the top, two rooks picked at a few stubborn apples that looked like knuckles. Further away, bright stone walls sheltered the grasses and dying herbs and briars from the cold breeze.

Granny and Grandad's house really suits them.

Across the stairs from my bedroom, Granny's window overlooks the street and her bed shakes with the passing traffic. On my side of the stairs, Grandad's bedroom window faces out on his hilly land – and even from here you can see over to the corner of Bluebell's little field.

Yawning, I stretched out and touched the blue ribbon on the wall with my fingers. She hadn't even shown any sign of tiredness after the showing class. But I had given her an extra feed last night. Grandad was well pleased with her getting second prize, even if there were only five ponies in the class.

He did say that the judge knew very little about horses – that his father was a lot better judge. And I would say he was probably right.

It had been a good day. I felt under the pillow for the tenner prize-money Grandad had given me. Yes. A good day. Apart from not speaking to Mam on the phone. When she rang again, Dad could give her the news.

I stretched again. Today, I could go to town and shop.

It was peaceful here. I could see out over the back lawn

57

and down to the trees at the end. That was another thing that was different here – the trees. Just now, the scraggy conifers with the sun brightening their tops looked snug and safe, screening the fruit trees from the wind as they stirred about. But when the wind blew hard, they groaned and cried. A crow flapped from them. Big and black, he opened his stony beak. I clapped my hands and he flew off in a fluster.

'Sarah, you stay warm in bed until I put down the fire.' Grandad must have heard me in the kitchen underneath, his footsteps matter-of-fact, going about his morning chores. I lay there listening to the morning sounds. Loud raking of the ashes sent shivers of soot into my bedroom fireplace. The porch door was unlocked and he pottered around to the back. The thud of the bin-lid. Smell of toast wafting up the stairs.

I snuggled under the clothes again and opened *The Complete Book of Survival,* on loan from the school library. 'What should you do if abducted ... Stay calm and quiet ... Pick out clues as to where the kidnapper is taking you ... '

Dad popped his head in and was gone again. More old cronies.

'I'll get them for you, Gran.' Kneeling in front of the warm range I dragged her shoes out from under it. She took off her slippers.

'Good girl.' Grandad at the table, wearing his tea-cosy, poured some hot water into a saucer. 'Granny, don't touch that fire with the poker or you'll put it out.' He took a small slurp out of the saucer. 'Ahhh,' and the steam rose out of him. 'Sarah, will you eat something. God help us, you're fierce thin.'

'What other way would she be when she's growing so fast? Did you take your tablets?' Granny's head turned to him, fingers working on her long wispy hair, winding it into a bun.

'Don't bother me about tablets.' Grandad beckoned me to the chair beside him.

I told him I wanted a boiled egg. 'I love the taste of the eggs here.'

'All right. Hand me out the small saucepan. The eggs ye get in Dublin are not the same at all.' He shuffled about, craning his neck to see the clock over the mantelpiece. 'Is that clock right, Granny? Give it five minutes.'

'Salt.' He topped the egg. Hand outstretched. 'Butter – where's the butter? Now, taste that.' Standing to attention at my elbow.

'Delicious.'

He offered me the top off his own free-range egg. Finished, he got up. 'I have to let out the dog and then take a walk up to Bluebell.'

I'm coming with you,' I said.

But Granny had a job for me. 'Wait a while, Sarah. I want you to go to the shop.'

Grandad said, 'Do the shopping first, so. After the dinner you and I will go up to her and give her a thorough examination. Now, can you give me a hand with this tie.'

His tie was so limp I could only make a very small knot in it. 'Turn down that collar. Thanks. The rheumatism is catchin' me.' He groaned.

'Tight enough?' Lacing one black boot for him, then the other. He stamped them on the floor and stood up quickly. He is still lively in the legs. He's pretty careful about what he wears for the outdoors when he has jobs to do and is expecting bad weather. He believes in insulation.

Firstly, he shrugged into the old jacket of his greyish suit. That fitted tightly over his waistcoat and under the stained green quilted gilet with the fleece peeking out in the place where it had torn. Then he squeezed on his Crombie greatcoat over all. 'Feel the weight of that. Great heat in it. I have it for years.'

Granny muttered something that I couldn't catch.

All buttoned up, zipped up and bulging, Grandad's fingers fought with his fawn-coloured scarf that Granny calls 'a relic'. He looked deadly in his layers. Lastly, whisking off the tea- cosy, with a flick he landed it neatly on top of the press by the range and took down his brimmed felt hat off the frame of the picture of the Sacred Heart where it always hung. 'Be back for the dinner.' He disappeared into the porch.

Granny sent me hurrying out after him. 'Grandad, your pills. Granny says you forgot to take them, Grandad.'

'They're no use.' Stick in hand, he fumbled at the door latch. 'I don't take them any more. Give me terrible indigestion.' His mouth scrunched up in a deadly grin.

'Grandad, you're supposed to. They're for your bad heart.'

'Bad heart!' The red colour spread from under his collar into his face. 'My heart is perfect. Don't mind what Granny tells you. She thinks the doctors know everything when they know nothin'. It gives a bit of a jump now and then when I'm in bed. That's all. Anyway, the tablets are lost.'

He grabbed the dog-collar. 'Tell her to keep down that fire,' he said over his shoulder. 'But make sure she doesn't have too big a blaze or she'll burn the house.'

Granny sent me up to his room. His tablets were not on the little table beside his bed with the crucifix, his rosary-beads, his packets of mints and his transistor radio. I searched about his bed. Probably on top of the wardrobe.

Granny was calling me to go to the shop so I galloped downstairs.

When I got back, Grandad was putting on his hat. 'I'm just taking another walk up the land. I saw a couple o youngsters on the wall of the far field this morning and you wouldn't know what mischief they'd get up to, when they see a little pony. Do you want to come with me?'

'Well, I ...'

'Leave her.' Granny was clearing cups off the table. 'But take that dog with you. He burrowed into my flower-beds again this morning.'

'Of course I'll take Suki. He's the best friend I have here

all the year round,' and he went off.

Later, I helped Granny to thatch a little house. She was putting in an entry for an ICA competition: 'A Gift for A Tourist'. I hammered blades of straw until they were flat and glued them on to the sod of turf. As we worked, drops of rain blew against the window.

'Grandad will be drenched.' I felt worried about something.

'Huh, there's no fear of him. He has plenty of shelter in the hayshed. Put more briquettes on the fire there, like a good girl.'

I could hardly hear her now above the noise of the rain on the window pane. The trees at the end of the garden were swishing and swaying and bending so low they seemed to almost touch the roof of the house with their angry tossing. The hedge was being pulled asunder; it looked like the springy grey hair of an old man caught in a rage.

Running feet. It was Dad back from town. 'It's fairly wet out there. I'll be down in a minute.' He went upstairs to change.

I still felt sort of worried but didn't know why. After all, Bono was safe in Tooten Hill with Mam and Miranda, and Bluebell could get shelter if she wanted it. And Grandad could rest against the bales in the hayshed. A gust of wind blew ashes on to the kitchen floor and Granny closed the front of the range.

I watched *Home and Away* and the next time I looked, the wind and rain had stopped.

'Granny, I'm going to walk up to the field to see Bluebell.'

Granny glued the last piece of thatch on to her house. 'Wear your coat. The clouds are still very black looking ... ' She broke off. Someone was thumping on the front door. She hurried out and I followed.

It was Grandad. His face was the colour of ashes. He swayed on his feet. Dad and the garda helped him on to

the couch in the sitting-room and he lay there with his eyes closed.

'He was sitting on the footpath with the dog … he waved me down,' the garda said.

While Dad phoned for the doctor, Granny loosened his tie and shirt buttons, kneeling beside him. hands moving quickly, spreading open the wings of his boots as if somehow his real colour was trapped in there, ready to fly out. 'His pills,' she said. 'Get his pills.'

Racing back downstairs, I heard the ambulance's siren sounding outside on the road. Granny grabbed the tablets and closed the door. Minutes later Grandad was carried out on a stretcher. The doctor said quietly to Granny, 'His pulse is very weak. Almost undetectable. He many not survive the journey.'

Standing on the road with all the neighbours watching the ambulance pull away, no one spoke. It seemed as if what had happened was so gianormous it would fill our minds for ever and ever, with each of us lost in it for ever and ever, never being able to find ourselves again. Ever.

Dad got into his car to drive after the ambulance to the hospital but Granny didn't want to go. She gripped my arm. 'Suki,' she said quickly. 'Where's Suki? Get her, Sarah.'

Bluebell met me at the field gate with an alert enquiring look. Gently she nudged my shoulder, the smell of wet grasses on her warm breath close to my face. Then she dropped her head and walked slowly away, unperturbed. Hand on her wither, I felt her comforting strength as she sifted through Grandad's old weeds to find the herbs she wanted. There was no sign of Suki anywhere.

'Any news from the hospital, Granny?'

I helped her light the fire again while she told me. Dad had rung to say that Grandad was resting in Intensive Care and Suki was safe. The porter had taken her into the security hut until she could be brought home. Grandad wasn't able to talk very well. He had mumbled something about chasing boys out of Bluebell's field.

Granny's black rosary-beads ran rapidly between her fingers. 'Remember, Sarah, we're old now and we've our lives over us. We have to be ready when God calls us.'

Going up the stairs, the hot-water bottle felt very heavy. Even in bed, I couldn't stop thinking of Grandad fighting off those boys. On his own, waving his stick to defend Bluebell, with no one to help him. I should have been there by his side, instead of watching telly. Grandad thought they would harm my pony. His heart had broken.

Granny said we had to be ready when God called. But Grandad was not ready. And no matter how loudly God called, Grandad would pretend not to hear. He wasn't planning on going yet. No way. Who'd look after his cattle and sheep? Look after Suki? Definitely no way.

Anyway, how could that be fair? God calling Grandad for such a long journey all on his own?

The trees in the garden were crying. Sounds of someone

poking feebly at the fire. When I heard a bark, I knew it was Suki and Dad and I ran downstairs.

Granny made a bed for Suki with Grandad's old coats beside the range.

In the morning, passing by Grandad's room, I thought I heard him call me. Just a heap of old threadbare sheets and blankets. No one was allowed to 'make' his bed.

Downstairs, Dad was on the phone to Mam. He was saying we'd have to stay another day or two. Could she ring school and the laboratory? I made a sign that I didn't want to speak to her.

Suki was lying by the range and when I left to go up to the field, she came with me. After giving the old bread and carrots to Bluebell I made sure to lock the gate again before returning to the house.

Granny was talking in a solemn voice to Dad.

'Sarah.' Her eyes looked black.

Suddenly I was sweating. The room was hot and close. I waited to hear that Grandad was dead. But she was smiling now.

'He wants to see us.' Then my leg started going like crazy, like as if it was spring-loaded and I was really looking forward to telling Grandad about Suki and Bluebell because it would put him in top form.

'Hiya, Grandad.'

He rolled his eyes to look up at us and I stood, unsure. Here in the ward he looked different from the old Grandad. Sort of peeled and shiny-looking, like an onion, lying almost vertical in his nest of pillows.

But Granny went over to him – then she did an unexpected thing. She leaned down and kissed him. I'd never seen them kiss before and this was just like in the Sleeping Beauty because his mouth opened and he said, 'It's too late now.' It was Grandad all right. He breathed out a sorrowful sigh, hands folded on his chest. He looked very peaceful.

Granny said, 'I brought you a fresh pair of socks.' She rummaged in her bag and took out his grey hand-knitted ones and left them on the bed.

'Good. My feet get cold.' Then he saw me. 'Sarah! Come over here to me. Ah! It's lovely to see you. That man over here had his grandchildren in today, all around the bed, kissin' and huggin' him and I felt lonely.' His voice faded but grew strong again. 'In the ambulance, I could hear the siren blaring. I thought I was in a helicopter. And you know what? I felt the warm licks on the back of my hand. Wasn't Suki there in the ambulance with me. Doesn't that beat everything?'

'Were the boys chasing Bluebell, Grandad?' I asked him.

'Them blackguards ... she could have run against the wall. Lucky I had my big stick. They won't try that again! The key. Oh, Granny gave it to you. Good. Mind it for me.' He lay back on the pillows, breathing faster. 'And make sure she has water to drink. Fix that pillow under my head there.' Reaching behind him, he grasped the back of the bed and slowly hauled himself up higher. Through thin lips, 'How's Suki now?'

'She comes up to the field with me. She's fine.'

This was a welcome piece of news for him. His eyes grew watery at the memory of her. 'There's great nature in that dog. The best dog in Ireland.'

He said suddenly in an annoyed voice, 'Look over at Granny. She comes in to see me and spends the time talkin' to everybody else.' He stopped. 'Are you thirsty? There's plenty of 7-Up and Lucozade there.' His eyes twisted towards the drinking glass on his locker. 'I took out my teeth because they were hurtin' me. Could you give them a bit of a wash?'

The look of them floating in the water caused a funny feeling in my tummy, but not like when I'm hungry. Spilling off the water into the sink and gripping the pink gummy part I brushed away the mush stuck between them, first the top ones, then the bottom jaw.

I gave them back to him and his hand fumbled near his mouth. Then he gave a mighty grin; he looked better, more like the old Grandad. 'Ah, I feel great now. I like to have them in for visitors. Who's this?'

A nurse stopped by the bed. 'What would you like for lunch, Mr Quinn?'

When she'd gone, Grandad leaned over to Granny. 'Those nurses are pure saints. Walking saints.'

Granny helped him to change his socks. His feet looked ghostly even before Granny rubbed on the talcum powder.

After helping him with his new slippers and his dressing-gown we all walked together down the corridor, Grandad shuffling beside me.

'My first time to walk out. I feel great, thank God.'

'I'm glad I was allowed in to see you,' I said. 'I was afraid you might be dead.'

Grandad halted. He looked at me. Shock, then amazement chased each other across his face. 'What! Me dead!' He smiled as if I'd said something silly. 'Child, I couldn't die! Sure, I'm not eighty yet!'

Still, now that Grandad was better – the doctors said it was more of a weakness than a heart attack but that he would have to be careful – I would be glad to get back to my own home tomorrow. I thought Bluebell would too because she would have more company. I was wondering how Mam had got on with Miranda. She told Dad it would be great to have me back. Was she missing me?

I had been glad of the few days away. Then it struck me – maybe God had sent Grandad the weakness so that I wouldn't have to go back so soon.

I didn't sleep so well, just thinking about it and all.

8 BACK HOME

Bono welcomed us at the gate with loud barks. It was clear from his fat tummy that someone had been feeding him well. Too well. Miranda should be more careful with a labrador ...

Mam met us, all smiles.

My mouth fell open in shock. 'Mam, what did you do to your hair?'

She patted her new sleek hair. 'Miranda cut and styled it – do you like it?' She didn't wait for me or Dad to answer. Instead she rushed on, 'And she's a wonderful artist. Really talented. You should see her animal portraits. She got that talent from Auntie Mary. Grand-aunt Tess too, Lord have mercy on her.'

Aunt Tess and her landscapes! What was Mam talking about? She hated them. She'd put them in the little loo.

'Always very good with her hands. Wonderful what's in the genes. And we took Bono to the canal and he had a swim. He loved it.'

I suddenly felt sick after the journey. Maybe I'd picked up a bug in the hospital. Mam's voice was making me feel worse, going on and on about nothing. She'd never even thought of asking me about the show and about Bluebell's prize.

I cut in. 'Did Paula ring?'

'Yes. She came over. With Adrian, of all people. They all got on very well together. I think Miranda gave Paula a few tips about riding Tanoli ...'

For God's sake! Paula! And Adrian – what did he want?

She suddenly frowned. 'There's Yaqoub, of course.

Miranda does seem to like him a lot ...'

I dumped my things and ran out to Bluebell. To relax after the journey, she rolled on the grass and scratched her cheeks and neck on her favourite patch of earth.

I was glad to be back in my own space too. I put my new rosette up on my bedroom wall beside all my rosettes and my D-Test Certificate and the photos of me and Paula and Blackie and Bluebell. Pity we hadn't got a proper tack-room where people could see it.

'Sarah, it's Paula on the phone.'

'I've been ringing all day,' Paula said. She didn't sound at all as if she'd missed me. 'Is Miranda gone? She schooled Tanoli for me yesterday and he went really well for her. You know he doesn't make friends easily. When will she be coming to stay again? Adrian keeps asking about her. He's being nice to me so that I'll put in a good word for him.' She giggled on the far end.

So Miranda had made friends with her too. The words just slipped out. 'You never asked me to ride Tanoli.'

Paula said, 'Well, she's had wide experience with all kinds of horses at the riding centre, you know.' Paula sounded defensive.

'Yeah, well ...' I changed the subject. 'We had to stay on an extra few days because Grandad got a heart attack, a weakness, actually.'

'Yeah.' Her voice was concerned. 'Once my cousin had a horse with a bad heart. He had to get a tube inserted so that he could breathe and he's still alive.'

She had news. Mrs M was holding an indoor show at the weekend. 'It's just a little show. It might be very good experience for our ponies. Niall and Trevor are going too.'

I was glad to be back in my own bed. I took out my fancy paper, intending to write to Grandad but Dad came in and we prayed to Jesus, Mary and Joseph to give him back his health and strength.

'Grandad is over the worst. Now go to sleep. You and Paula have lots of things planned for tomorrow.'

Paula would be here early. For more roadwork, with
Paula time-checking us on stretches of road, timing us
between telegraph poles. I heard myself sighing. Paula
thought that Tanoli had improved at tracking and in
extended trot. Bluebell probably had too. But we hadn't
practised any jumping.

Something else was bugging me. Paula, and her being
friendly with Miranda. I couldn't care less about Adrian.

Bluebell halted on the road and she whinnied. She was
looking over the hedge into the bare field. There were
usually cattle in it. Today they were gone.

Then I spotted that the briary hedge was squashed
down. 'Wow! That's a deadly bank!' There was a running
stream inside.

'Come on, Paula. We have to do this!' I urged Bluebell
up to it and she responded willingly.

'Well, Tanoli can't do it. You shouldn't do it either. It's
too slippy. And if Mrs M comes out, there will be trouble.'

But Bluebell stepped gently into position and jumped.
We cleared it beautifully. I jumped her out on to the road

again. 'You try it now, Paula. It's great for tendons and muscles.'

'Leave it, Sarah. Come on.'

This time, Bluebell sprang from the margin. She skimmed the tops of the briars but skidded as we landed, falling on her knees and on her outstretched neck. I was thrown to the ground but wasn't hurt. She scrambled to her feet and shook herself. Her neck and front were coated with clay.

'Are you all right? Quick, use the gate.'

'I can't leave it like that. She has to do it again and do it better.' Determined that she should do it, I sat up once more, and walked Bluebell through the muck. She gathered herself and leaped lightly up on to the far bank.

'Would you hurry? What's the matter?' Up ahead, Paula was waiting for us to catch up.

'She's walking a bit funny.'

'She's probably sore after that fall.'

'No. I think she's lame. I'll have to take her home.' I got down.

'Maybe she's sprained a tendon,' Paula said. 'That will take months to heal.'

Dad was at the gate. He stood up to watch her as we walked past. 'She's lame all right. It's obvious in her walk. It's the left foreleg.' He picked it up. 'It seems a little hotter than the others. But don't worry about it, Sarah. She'll be fine. You go on inside now and I'll untack.' He had already opened the girth and was slipping off the saddle. 'I'll bet that lameness will be healed by morning.'

9 DROP IN THE HOOF

'Dad, Bluebell is hardly able to walk!' Grabbing at his sleeve. 'Come out. Now!' I couldn't keep the shake out of my voice.

Lip-reading me in the mirror he turned off his electric shaver and followed me to the stable.

'Was it Tuesday she was shod? It might be a problem with shoes – or nails. Her hoof is still a bit hot, but not very … ' He wiped his hands on the old stable rubber. 'Ring the farrier and tell him to come over right away.'

But Niall said his dad had already left to shoe horses at the Curragh. 'We'll call up as soon as he gets home. I'm sure she'll be okay.'

Bluebell had tumbled over that big ditch after I had made her jump it. It was my fault. She rested her sore foot and whinnied at me. Her head and ears were drooped.

'Mam, I told you, I'm not hungry.'

'It's not serious.' She sat beside me.

'Look, it could be a broken tendon.'

'She's not that lame.'

'She is, Mam. I know.' Pushing her away. There was a film over my eyes. I had seriously injured my pony just for the thrill of hunting her over a massive ditch.

Mam called after me, 'I phoned Chris Beresford. His locum should be here any minute.'

When the sparkling two-tone jeep screeched to a stop on the driveway, Bono chased into the field and barked at Bluebell but she didn't move.

'Is this Quinn's?'

Speaking sharply to Bono, the grumpy-looking vet tried

71

to wipe the pawmarks off his white trousers. He studied Bluebell, drumming his fingers on the gate. Picking up her hoof he rooted around the frog with his hoof-pick. 'It's a hoof infection.'

But when I asked him what kind of an infection it was and what might have caused it, he dropped the hoof. 'Bloody Hell. What do you think I am? I'm a veterinary surgeon, not a horse whisperer ... can you not hold that animal? He's so awkward.'

'It's a mare.'

'Mares are worse. She must be in season.'

Bluebell turned her head.

'Ouch!' He swore some more and rubbed his bum. 'Oh hell. Tell the farrier to remove that shoe. I'll give her an antibiotic and a tetanus shot. That'll be thirty-five pounds.'

I rubbed Bluebell's head to comfort her.

A figure was walking up from the gate.

'Hi.'

'Oh, Miranda. I thought you were Paula.'

Miranda said she had got a lift up from the riding centre; Mam must have told her about Bluebell. 'Let's have a look.'

First she circled Bluebell's head, then knelt down beside her in the grass and began to stroke her face and eyelids, sweeping her hand over them, shading them. Bluebell rested with her neck and head flat on the ground as she was stroking her

Then I noticed the bag of tools she had with her, like Willie's. She explained, 'I borrowed them at the riding centre. I really won't be doing this until my A-Test.'

'But you don't know how.'

'Don't worry. I've seen Mrs M and the farrier do it and I've helped them lots of times. Got lessons on care and management of the foot too.' She broke off. 'Whoa, there, pet. I'm not going to hurt you.'

She snipped off the clinches and removed the shoe, then

showed me the sole of the hoof, even as Bluebell tried to pull it free. 'That's sore and there's heat in it. It's a drop-in-the-hoof, I would think. She got a prod. A sharp stone could have done it.'

I watched nervously as Miranda caught the hoof between the pincers. She worked her way around the hoof, squeezing the sole underneath, trying for the tender spot. Suddenly Bluebell jerked her leg away. Miranda sat back on her hunkers. 'I've found it.'

She got her paring-knife and using the blade with the slight hook on the top she firmly pared until she had formed a slight hole.

'Now, if I'm lucky, this should do it.' There was a small jet of pus. She made a bigger puncture, working slowly and carefully. Bluebell pushed her head back and stretched out her big bulk contentedly. I murmured softly to her and stroked her eyes like I'd seen Miranda do.

'Look.' Miranda took away her hand. The yellow stuff was oozing steadily out of the hole. It smelled awful. 'It's draining well,' she said with satisfaction.

'You poor pony,' I soothed.

We stood well clear as Bluebell staggered to her feet. Next thing she was breaking wind into my face, sounding like an air-balloon. I stopped laughing when I saw her put her head on Miranda's shoulder. 'She'll dirty your sweat-shirt,' and I swung Bluebell's head back towards me.

Miranda didn't seem to notice. She bent down and searched in her bag. With a knife, she smeared the treacly tar on to the piece of cotton wool and packed the hole.

The farrier's blue car gurgled up the driveway and Niall got out – followed by Trevor! I waved at them. Niall was helping his dad take the equipment out of the car and Trevor was kicking stones and grabbing at Bono, app-earing very casual. Just think! he had come all this way to see Bluebell.

I called out, 'Bluebell is going to be okay. Miranda found the drop-in-the-hoof.'

She gestured towards the hoof and asked Willie to have a look at it.

Speaking in a low voice, I explained to Trevor and Niall what she had done to the hoof. 'Wow!' Trevor breathed.

After inspecting it, Willie took off his leather apron and said to Miranda, 'You got it, all right. But that pus in the hoof must drain away completely.' He advised us to keep Bluebell in the stable for the time being.

Now Trevor was bending down beside my pony. He was peering at the hoof and sighing. He really seemed so sorry for Bluebell. Niall asked me to give him a hand and I helped him to carry the box of tools to the car while his father was talking to Mam at the back door.

Niall said, 'Dad said Miranda did a good job. She's pretty cool ... I wonder...' he kicked the ball for Bono who bounded off after it.

'Wonder what?

'Do you think she could cure a pony's eye infection too?'

'Wait there.' I shot past Trevor, still talking to Miranda, and slipped into the house. Back again, I threw the plastic bag at Niall. 'They're Gold Blend. The best.'

'Gee, thanks.' He clutched them and called to Trevor to hurry on. Trevor shouted, 'Do you think there would be room in the car for Miranda?'

'Sure.'

Miranda smoothed her jodhpurs. 'Actually, that would be great. I've got to get back to Castleknock. I'll just say good-bye to my mom first.'

Trevor said, 'We can wait, can't we, Niall?' Was he blind and deaf? Did he not see Willie waving and shouting at them to hurry on?

Miranda left the tin of ointment with me after telling me when to apply it. Trevor lifted her bag of tools into the car. Last thing, I heard Niall telling her about his pony's eye infection and asking her to take a look.

'Wow! How did she do it?' Paula gently lowered Bluebell's

foot as I explained how Miranda had found the drop-in-the-hoof. 'Cool! I wish I'd been here!' She seemed very impressed. Why couldn't I feel the same?

Bluebell nosed at Tanoli for sympathy and understanding but the big pony lifted his head clear in the air. As if he didn't care much about Bluebell's misfortune.

Thistledown and dog hairs whirled in the soft sunshine at the corner of the house. The leaves were thinning in the quickthorn hedges bordering the empty paddock.

I was attending to Bluebell in the stable, feeding and mucking-out, mucking-out and feeding her, bathing her wound in Jeyes Fluid and pasting on the Stockholm tar.

That meant I'd very little free time to spend with Miranda. Her visits were short, what with school and the riding centre and homework and Yaqoub and all. From the stable I could hear her and Mam talking and laughing together. And Miranda's loud rock music that she listens to. Smell the cigarette smoke in the green room which is

now hers, though she never stays overnight. Her other mother usually honks the car horn from the gate when she comes to collect her. I love the sound of that horn.

Bluebell loved the smell of the tar. It was helping her injury to heal. I could see she was in better form. But every morning recently as I was leaving her for school, she scratched her jaw on the half door.

'She's probably bored out of her mind,' Niall said when I told him. He brought in an old leather horse boot to protect the wound from mud and dirt while she walked about. Paula helped me to strap it on her leg and I led her out for a short graze.

That day, as I opened the gate into the field, something unusual happened. When Tanoli strode forward to go through first, Bluebell pecked him on the flank. He didn't argue with her. Respectfully stepping aside he let her through.

I didn't get a chance to tell Paula – she rode home soon after, her sight being a bit wonky with her bad headache. I expect she didn't see how my bossy-boots had checked Tanoli.

My fork heaped shavings into the barrow. At the hunt, the other horses would let her through first too. We wouldn't be disgracing ourselves by trailing at the back of the field. She knew what to do herself.

I grabbed the saddle soap from the biscuit box in the porch. The smell of soft leather filled my face as the creamy paste soaked into the cracks. I could see her through the hedge, grazing quietly. I rubbed harder.

Just wait. We'd be leaping the ditches again before very long. Her injury was just an accident. It happens to every horse once. So the farrier said. And Miranda ... well, I would have to be careful.

Whatever happened, she was not going to take Bluebell – or my friends – away from me.

10 LESSONS

These are pet days. The sun is warm and a clump of dog-daisies glows beside the red fuchsia. Spiders scuttle on the high wire from the wall of the house to a leafy bush, bridging the path with shining webs of steel. At night, the moon fails to come out until it is pitch-dark and then it hangs big and orange down low in the sky.

I was still not too happy about the show. I tried to tell Paula when we were out on the hack, but she had gone too far ahead on Tanoli. I could barely see them. Then something unexpected happened. A band of silent riders came trotting towards us out of the mist.

Miranda was in the lead on a big grey horse called Bruno, one of the livery horses at Mrs M's. About to pass me, she spoke in her put-on riding-school voice, not stopping. 'Sarah, the arena will be free at four o'clock tomorrow. I'll give you a jumping lesson if you like.' They trotted on and I sat there on Bluebell looking after them.

Paula rode back to me to hear what she'd said.

I gabbled, 'She wants to give me a riding-lesson.'

'Lucky you,' Paula said. Her face was still pale after her headache. 'I wish I'd been given that chance.'

'But I don't want any lessons. Bluebell is doing fine. I'd prefer just hacking out with you.'

Paula said firmly, 'Go for it. She's experienced. She'll probably do some gymnastic jumping with you. It'll improve your riding and make Bluebell more responsive to you and more supple.'

'But what about hacking out together ... '

'We can still do that – after the lesson. Then you can fill me in.'

'Thanks, Paula.' As we rode on through the mist, Tanoli in the lead again, I felt more cheerful. I thought more and more that Paula was right. Roadwork was very good but Bluebell certainly needed some jumping experience before the show. The lesson would provide that. And hacking out after the lesson would relax Bluebell, and, most important, I wouldn't miss out on being with my best friend.

I wanted the lesson. But not with Miranda.

I know I'm going to be stiff and sore after the day. The lesson Miranda gave me was based on one she had seen Gerry Mullins give in the riding centre.

Beforehand, she'd explained, 'Jumping is technical. It's about timing and pacing, counting your strides coming into the jumps.' She would teach me to approach the fences safely and correctly. And teach my pony to jump in the correct shape.

We had begun by working on our circles, which she said were less than perfect, more pear-shaped. To improve them, she got me to use my forward seat to help Bluebell loosen her back muscles before going back to my normal seat. And after that, Bluebell did large loops, serpentines, circles and changes of direction until I was dizzy from all the twists and turns – and I have to say she did them better than ever. That part of the lesson went well. Now Bluebell was in the mood for working.

We had gone on to the ground rails and small gymnastic jumping exercises. Miranda placed ground poles at four feet six inches apart that led to a small fence nine to ten feet from the last pole. Again she explained that this would allow Bluebell to stretch her neck, looking down to the ground with a rounded body outline; this helped to develop the pushing power from her hind legs.

Trot, trot, trot. Count five strides – 5-4-3-2-1. An echo in my head. 'Put in six this time.'

I pictured Miranda again, leaping up on Bluebell after she had gone flying down over the trotting poles, nearly falling, and then bolting with me, wanting to get away from the muddle. Trot, trot, trot. Miranda had pulled on Bluebell's back teeth, holding her back. Trot, trot, trot, holding her back again, showing her what to do.

Bluebell hadn't thought she could do it. She would never be the same again. I patted my pony. She'd had to work hard and could now enjoy hacking out as a break from the serious schooling, even though it was still an important part of our fitness programme.

'Sorry, Paula.' She was waiting for me at the gate. The lesson had taken longer than I'd expected. 'Have you ever done canter poles, Paula?'

'Yeah, that's a bit advanced.'

'It wasn't perfect but it's something to work on.'

Paula said, 'Well, it wouldn't matter a dead dog's breakfast out hunting.' Tanoli sprinted ahead on the road.

I caught up with her and explained the lesson and Paula at last slowed down and listened, frowning in concentration. 'She's taking me for another lesson tomorrow.'

'Lucky you.'

At next lesson, we went through the same drill. We had to trot over six trotting poles. Trot, trot, until the trot over the poles was regular, then canter the right number of strides to the cross-poles jump that was set up directly behind the trotting poles, adding on another pole, building up Bluebell's concentration and her tempo.

Miranda's lessons would help to make Bluebell and me more alert, explaining how to approach the jumps. She would show me ways of taking better control between fences and help Bluebell to gauge a better approach into the jump; and Bluebell would listen and respond to my seat and legs and my voice, and lengthen or shorten her strides going into a jump. We'd both know the right place to 'take-off' ... not too far or too near the fence, causing it to fall. Regulate the trot and canter into the jump.

Regulate the transitions between jumps. Get the tempo and cadence right for the perfect jump. That should be a big help for the hunt.

Later, on our hacks out together, I would be out of breath explaining to Paula as she listened intently. Paula would memorise all of it for when Tanoli started jumping.

But right now she was going to be disappointed. 'Sorry, Paula. Miranda asked me to hack out with her tomorrow after my lesson.'

'That's okay.' Paula shrugged. 'She'll be riding Bruno, won't she? He is a bit fresh and Tanoli would only get upset.' Her voice sounded thin. 'I wish I had an older sister who could coach me, instead of that eejit Adrian. He's so dumb – keeps phoning Miranda trying to make a date with her. You'd think he'd get the message.'

And what did I think of Miranda now? I had to admit she was good with Bluebell, patient but firm and took no nonsense from her. And Bluebell was more alert and responsive to me since she had begun to help with our training. And being friends with her was certainly easier since all that talk of her coming to live with us had died down.

As soon as I got back from Mrs M's, I rang Paula to tell her what happened.

After hacking out, I'd gone back with Miranda to the yard and met Yaqoub. He knew who I was straightaway. 'So you're Sarah, the little sister.' He'd put his hand under Bluebell's chin and said she was 'smashing' and that she looked really stylish in the numnah. The earring was gone from his forehead.

Bluebell liked him and so did I. She nearly ate the Star Trek badge off his jumper.

'I think he suits Miranda better than Adrian,' I told Paula.

Paula didn't comment. 'Will you be able to hack out with me tomorrow?'

'Yeah, I suppose so.' I tried to sound enthusiastic.

But, really, it was more fun with Miranda. She was better able to control her horse and keep in stride. And, she let Bluebell go ahead. 'It's good for her to take the lead,' she'd said.

'You can put your pony in here.' Miranda opened the stable door.

I was getting to know the older girls working in the yard and when we were having tea together in Mrs M's kitchen, I told them about Grandad's dog travelling with him in the ambulance and how she saved him with her licks. They thought Suki was great. They were all laughing, including Miranda, and I could see she was pleased with me.

Miranda stubbed out her cigarette. She never smokes around the horses or in the stables. 'Okay. Back to work.' She was in charge and she linked my proud arm as we went off together.

But that first time riding out on Mrs M's cross-country course was scary. Miranda went in front on big Bruno. With me leaning back in the saddle to balance her, Bluebell followed down the three banks into the water and dropped carefully up to her belly. Then it wasn't scary any more. She could nearly swim in it. Splash! Lucky I had swopped my jodhpur boots for my rubber boots, as Miranda had advised me.

Bluebell was getting more adventurous and so was I. She was well muscled, fit and well fed – Miranda had advised less grass and more nuts.

On the day we hacked out with Niall and Trevor I could feel Bluebell's new air of confidence. I'd told Niall we might be taking in the cross-country and they met up with us. We clattered up the road together, like in a cowboy film. After we turned into the cross-country field we realised the ground was very wet and Miranda decided we would not jump. Instead, we swung out across the field, and trotted, four abreast, like a regiment in the cavalry.

God, I thought, if Bluebell could get so enthused in the company of three others, what was she going to be like in a field of seventy or eighty horses and ponies!

Meanwhile, Paula was hoping that Tanoli would soon be fit enough for hunting and for cross-country events. 'His tendons are much stronger, and with more roadwork he should last the pace.'

Bluebell put on a spurt. 'Yeah. Great. But you haven't ridden over fences ... '

'Well, Mrs M did advise flatwork for one whole month. But you know I can't wait to go jumping again.'

I was sorry she was missing out, but it wouldn't be for long, the way Tanoli was shaping up. And the show was coming up at the weekend. And the hunt at mid-term.

I was in bed early and almost asleep when the voices started, low at first, then getting louder. In the listening darkness.

'You would think she'd take a few hours off to visit her mother.'

Dad's voice: 'Miranda has her own life to live. Don't expect her to come running to you every free minute she gets. Remember the saying, "Your children are through you, but they are not yours." Anyhow, she and Sarah are getting on well together.'

Mam's voice again: 'Yes. But what about me? I'm her mother.'

I stuffed the duvet in my ears.

11 THE SHOW

In the paddock, goldfinches perched and fed on the swaying blacktops. The gooseberry bushes had grown twiggy and bleach brown. Red berries on the creepers blended with the last of the roses and stalky green nettles showed their heads through the hedge.

At first, Paula wanted to go in the dressage event with Tanoli, but then she changed her mind and decided to enter the Clear Round Jumping. This course was bigger than that which Bluebell and Blackie had faced at Kill Show in early summer a year ago. And now our ponics would have to jump two clear rounds before winning a rosette.

Paula had set this as the test for Tanoli. If he went well over these obstacles, she knew he would also go well for her at the hunt.

We didn't get a chance to inspect the course; the jumping competition itself had started by the time we got back from the dressage arena. Niall explained the layout to me. Seven jumps in all and the best of two rounds. I tried to concentrate.

The first fence was bales with a pole on top. Then an oxer – two poles on the same level; a hog's back – three poles, the two outer at the one level and the middle one higher; crossed poles; and a fan fence on the corner.

'Watch that wall, it's spooky.' A plywood wall with imitation stones painted on the surface. A lot of ponies were refusing at it.

Mam came over and said, 'That's a lovely course.' She

patted Bluebell but her eyes were elsewhere, searching for Miranda.

Paula was nearby, getting ready. She caught my eye and directed my gaze to Adrian who was attentively fixing her stirrup. Probably hoping Miranda would turn up.

'Hi.' Babs was grinning up at me. I felt better. Babs was here to cheer me on.

'Look.' I showed her my sweaty palms before drying them on my jodhpurs.

'Yeah. Good luck.' She fidgeted with Bluebell's mane, tugging at it. 'Is your mother not waiting to see you and Bluebell jumping?'

I noticed then that Mam was hurrying towards the entrance.

'She didn't really come for that – she's just looking about for Miranda.' At least Babs wasn't running after my sister.

Babs bounced about. 'Yeah. Maybe I have an older sister in Hollywood – with lots of money. Everyone says I look like Christine Rice? You know – the model?' She flicked the fringe out of Bluebell's eyes and Bluebell flinched at the sudden movement. Then, all of a sudden, Babs stood still and grinned at me. 'When you see Miranda, tell her … my place at four o'clock on Saturday. Me and Katie are holding a bit of a party …' She bounced about again.

'Am I not invited?'

She gave me a look that made me feel cold. There was a mixture of sadness and delight in her green eyes. She had found a way to hurt me again. 'I'm only allowed ask twenty-seven people. Miranda will be coming to live in your house soon and my mam says I have to introduce her to my friends.'

My whip was tapping against my boot and Bluebell shifted about in agitation. 'Miranda won't be living with us. She won't go to your party … she's too old …'

I noticed Paula signalling to me in the background and I heard my pony's name, the one she used at shows, over the public-address system. 'Windy Mountain will be ridden by

Sarah ...' Suddenly I could hardly hold the reins.

Then Miranda was at my side. She said, 'Shorten up those reins or she'll run out on you. Take a wide circle and give her a chance to see the fences.'

I trotted Bluebell into the arena and skirted around the fences to let her see the different obstacles. Then, when the bell went, I circled, just remembering to salute the judges, picked up canter on the right rein and went into the first jump, counting the strides as Miranda had taught me. Bluebell was enjoying herself. So was I.

'Oh no!' I should have got Miranda to put up a double for me during the week. My pony hadn't done a double for ages. Coming into it, she was looking around her. I gave her a tap of the stick. With that, she speeded up and out of stride, took a huge leap over the first part, which landed

her too close to the second part. She stopped dead but when I roared, 'Come on, Bluebell,' she jumped clear over the second part too. The 'wall' was the second last jump from the end and she took it and the last one without any real bother.

The second round was even better.

Niall rushed over to us. His pony had been eliminated at the wall. 'I can't believe it ... how Bluebell jumped that wall. She did it perfectly.'

'Well, she was born in Galway, you know.'

Tanoli sprang around and surprised a lot of people by jumping a double clear round too.

'You're in the shake-up. Only five of you got double clears,' said Miranda. 'Off you go.'

Mrs M was calling us into the centre of the arena. 'There's a prize of a lead rope for the rider who picks up the rosette with the cross on the back,' she said.

Niall grabbed my ribbon off me and held it up. There was the little blue biro mark.

'Fantastic.' I leaned over Bluebell's warm neck and hugged her.

I was hoping Miranda could come for tea. She said she'd like to. But first she had to ring her parents in Castleknock. She rang on her mobile phone while I tried to get Bluebell to stand quietly.

'What do you mean, I'm neglecting you? How?' She was frowning into the mouthpiece. She put it down abruptly. When Bluebell nudged her, she turned to me and said in a flat voice, 'Miranda, Miranda – I'm beginning to hate that name, though do I really want to be called after a hen ...?'

'What's wrong?' I said.

'They think I'm spending too much time here.'

I waited, then said, 'Are you allowed come to tea?'

She lifted the rake and strode off. 'I have to finish my chores first.' She had made up her mind to come, I could tell. I hurried away to Paula.

After, when we were walking our ponies back up the hill,

we couldn't keep our voices down. Paula said that Adrian trailed after Miranda all day, even helped her tack up when she was exercising Bruno. 'He's totally lunatic about her. Hey, did you know that Trevor's new pony used to be a Grade A jumper in the under 148 cms?'

'Yeah, he told me. But Tanoli is a natural jumper. It takes very little out of him. He'd jump anything.'

She giggled. 'I can't believe he jumped clear – he's had only one lesson.'

'Yeah, but I got the lead rope.' It was coiled up on my saddle.

Paula stopped laughing.

Mam drove past us with Miranda and I got Bluebell to walk faster.

'And there's me when I was a baby. I look really funny, don't I?'

Miranda looked hard at the family photo I was showing her. I was in Mam's arms with Dad beside me and we were all happy-looking and smiling. 'And there's my granny and grandad ...'

She got up and I made a grab for the photo album as it slid off the couch on to the floor.

Mam was putting away the tea-things and she looked up in surprise. 'You're not leaving already, Miranda. I thought we'd have a chat as soon as you'd finished looking at the album. We have hardly seen each other recently or spoken to each other.'

'What have we to talk about?'

'I wanted to hear how you were getting on school – Helen McDonnell said your teachers are concerned about you – that you're not working. You told me you were taking art as a subject for your Leaving Certificate and I did go to some trouble ordering those expensive art books for you. And now you want to give it up. I really don't think you should ... ' Her voice trailed off. 'Where are you going?'

Miranda was buttoning up her fleece jacket. 'I'm going back to my parents who looked after me when you abandoned me.'

Mam stood without moving, hands by her sides. 'You'll need a lift,' was all she said.

'I'll manage that. I'm not depending on you.' The door slammed with such force that Mam's cactus plant fell from the window-sill and went crashing down on to the tiles. Bits of pottery mixed with black clay were sprayed everywhere. As if in a daze, Mam knelt down and began to pick up the pieces.

'Miranda, wait!' I ran and caught up with her at the gate. 'Make sure you ring Mam. Please, Miranda.' Miranda didn't know how long Mam had spent cooking that awful dinner for her. If she had known she'd feel sorry for her.

She was panting and the rain glistened on her cheeks. 'If she wants, she can ring me. I'm the one always making the effort.'

'Miranda!' But she was gone.

Bluebell had come alongside the fence to investigate. I stroked her for a while to calm her, tell her everything was all right. Then I ran inside to help Mam sweep up the mess.

12 SHOPPING WITH MIRANDA

Down at the corner of the field the oak tree rustled feebly against the foggy sky. Midges hovered and swarmed into Bluebell's face over the damp leaves.

'When will Miranda be calling to your house again?'

I'd told Paula how Miranda had criticised the way she was riding Tanoli. But instead of being upset, it was the opposite. She said she wished she could have lessons too.

Anyway, there was no point in talking about it.

'She doesn't even ring Mam any more?' I said. Mam leaves messages for her to phone but she doesn't because the MacDonnells don't like it. They want her to study. Miranda told me.'

I remembered the last time Mam had rung and spoken to Mrs MacDonnell. When she put down the phone she was crying. I'd decided I hated Miranda's parents for making Mam unhappy. Miranda too. Why couldn't she be nicer to Mam?

Strange thing: next time Miranda rang, she wanted to talk to me.

It was the first time I'd been allowed to travel to town on my own. So, even though I had mixed feelings about Miranda – I mean I wasn't too happy about how she was treating Mam and all – I still felt as if I was going on an exciting adventure. She was waiting for me at the bus stop outside Bewleys, as she'd said.

'Mam gave me money to give you to buy us lunch.' I pulled out the purse to show her. 'We can go to Planet

Hollywood. Or anywhere you like. I'm easy.' And I had Grandad's tenner in my shoe for safe keeping, in case we got mugged. I had read about that somewhere. I wasn't sure what I was going to buy with it – yet.

'Hold on.' She shoved the money back into my purse. 'It's too early to eat. Let's do some shopping first.'

We walked around the shops. Miranda wanted to try on stuff. In Brown Thomas she strutted up and down in a slinky silver sequinned dress and grey fur coat topped off with a floppy hat.

'Gawd, Miranda, we'll be thrown out.'

I listened in amazement as the sales assistant enquired if she'd like to try the dress in a different size.

'No. It's not me. But I do like the hat – I'll take it.'

Now she was asking about a pair of high heels that would be suitable for a wedding. For me! She picked out a pair of gold strappy sandals and I put them on over my green Aran woolly socks. The assistant asked if I wanted pop socks but Miranda told her firmly, 'No. She'll be wearing these socks to the wedding.' I paraded up and down after she'd warned me to keep a straight face.

Paula and I would never have the guts to do this! I couldn't wait to tell her. This was great. No wonder she said she'd prefer to have an older sister than an older brother. 'Ugh!' Miranda pulled back from a hanger. 'Don't touch it,' she warned and showed me the label – £2,500. Passing the cosmetic counter, she stopped and, with a quick swipe of the mascara brush, left a big streak of copper Christian Dior in my hair.

'Now, you're gorgeous ... What do you think, Sarah?' She lowered the brim of the new hat over her eyes.

'Excellent.' She looked like a famous actress shopping incognito. We walked out of the shop, her arm cosy in mine. It was then I decided what I was going to buy with Grandad's tenner. And I knew where to get it. We walked up to Baggot Street and she waited outside the shop for me until I was ready.

Later, at the bus stop, foot on step, I turned to her. 'We had a great day, hadn't we, Mir? I hope we can go to town again soon. By the way, Mam wants you to come for tea tomorrow.'

'I can't.' Her voice was low under the hat. She stubbed out her cigarette. 'Sarah,' she hesitated, 'I won't be able to see you for a few weeks ... '

'Oh. Will you be able to come and stay at mid-term?' Then I told her about the party Mam was planning.

From the top of the bus, I waved down at the floppy hat as it wandered off through the crowd. I placed my packet carefully on the empty seat beside me.

Amazing. Mam didn't even ask me how we'd spent all the money. 'So you and Miranda had a good time?'

'She's so funny. We were in all the shops trying on all kinds of gear ... '

Mam interrupted, fingering the choker I'd made up in the bead shop. 'Will she be coming for tea tomorrow?'

'No, Mam. She has to give up working at the riding centre for a few weeks. She has an art project to do and her parents want her to finish it.'

Mam's fingers pulled at the beads so much I got worried she'd break my choker. 'What about her mid-term break?'

'I think her parents want her to spend it with them.'

The beads rattled back on the table and Mam stood up. Her fists were clenched. 'She'll be seventeen at Halloween. I want to be with my daughter for her seventeenth birthday.' She stopped. 'Did you tell her about the party?'

'Yes, but she didn't say anything. I don't think she likes parties ...'

Muttering to herself Mam went straight to the phone to ring Castleknock.

'You're not going on the Junior Hunt.' Mam was in rotten humour.

'But, Mam, you said I could go.'

'Miranda isn't a Green Coat any more. I can't be running along beside you for twenty miles. So the answer is no!'

'But Paula and Niall and Trevor are going. We'll be looking out for each other.'

'I said no.'

Angrily I stood in her path. 'I knew you'd say that. You never let me do anything. You're overprotecting me. Everything I do is too dangerous. Paula's mother lets her do what she likes and go where she likes. She never tells her when to come home, or when to do her homework.'

'She doesn't have to remind her. Paula just does it.'

But when I asked Dad about it, he said he didn't mind having to run along with me for twenty miles – he could do with the exercise. Now Mam had no excuse for not letting me go and she knew it.

When I met her, Paula sounded glum. Then she said, 'So Miranda isn't a Green Coat any more. God, they might be stuck for someone – maybe I should volunteer.'

She reined in Tanoli at the fence and I took a rest. She had important news to tell me. 'The Junior Hunt is meeting in Straffan on Sunday. We could hack there. Mom says she'll pay the subscription for me so I'm going, if Tanoli is fit enough.'

It would be Trevor's first hunt too. At computers, we talked the whole time about the height of the jumps and the big ditches and drains and the many miles of galloping across country.

Trevor said our ponies would have to have enough stamina to gallop flat out across fields and over fences for an indefinite length of time.

Niall was all for us practising together but Paula was not in favour. 'Tanoli would get a setback. He's only learning to calm down now,' she said.

'Bluebell won't have any problems with her stamina,' I said, and then told the others confidently. 'She could trot for ever without getting tired.'

But I had noticed that even though Tanoli got so excited at the start that he immediately sweated up; the funny thing was, he could stay going for ever.

Bluebell had got lazy again. Actually she wouldn't canter for me at all without a mighty effort.

'Look! This ditch is huge. I did it with Miranda.'

Bluebell pulled up and looked at it.

'I'll get up on her.' Paula got down off Tanoli and up on Bluebell. I pulled a stick out of the hedge and handed it to her. Bluebell fired her hind legs angrily into the air and with a fart she took off. Tanoli reared and I was dragged to the ground as he whizzed up the hill after her, like as if a wasp was on his tail.

Paula returned, red-faced. 'I think it's time for me to be going home.'

I brushed myself. 'Me too.'

It had been different with Miranda.

13 HALLOWEEN

The fog lay in wait at the edges of the wet fields and sometimes it lifted a little, then crept back again. But all the time it lay in wait, to pounce. At night, sharp frost seeped through the sloes and reddened haws and in the morning it dropped off the hedges.

Holding on to the head-collar, I ran beside Bluebell, keeping pace with her trot, Dad watching from behind.

'She looks really well ... whoa ...' She trotted through the muck to the gate and showered us with splatters. Rearing up, she boxed the air with her hooves and I had to grip on tightly to the rope to bring her back down to earth.

Dad laughed. 'She's certainly showing signs of her new fitness regime and the extra feeding.'

He held her while I ran off to answer the phone. It was Paula, with disappointing news.

'Dad, the Junior Hunt is cancelled in Straffan because of the rain last night. The land is flooded.'

This was a major disappointment. Next Sunday would have been ideal, being our mid-term break and not having any school on Monday, and we'd have had plenty of time to recover, even if we'd cracked a rib or something.

Dad said thoughtfully, 'Gweena will be coming up. She's collecting Strike at the horse hospital in Kildare. Maybe we could arrange something else ... '

Before I could ask him what he meant, he slapped Bluebell on the rump. 'Well, if you're going trick 'n' treating, you'd better get ready. Mam won't want you late for dinner tonight. Remember Miranda will be coming.'

Paula dipped the brush into the red paint and started on my cheeks. Slowly my appearance changed until I looked like an American Indian squaw. My leg began to dance.

Paula was talking about the hunt. 'There will probably be another hunt the following week.' She used the brush with determination, then handed me the face paints and I got to work on her.

Mam appeared in the doorway clutching some feathers. 'I found them on an old hat. They might be of some use to you,' and she went out humming.

'Your mam's in fabulous humour.'

'Yeah, for a change. She's really looking forward to seeing Miranda and she's ordered heaps of stuff for the birthday tomorrow. She's never been with Miranda for her birthday before.'

For some reason, I was kind of excited about the idea myself and I told Paula, 'I wanted to wait until night-time so that she could come trick 'n' treating with us, but Mam won't let me take Bluebell out on the road after dark.'

Paula said it would have been too late for her too. 'Mom is going out early and I have to baby-sit.'

'Pity ... Will you be coming to the party tomorrow? Mam said I could ask you.'

'Thanks, I'd love to. I won't have a present with me. Adrian owes me money so I'll have to wait to get it.'

'That's okay. She'll get heaps. A lot of Mam's relations are coming and Gweena might be here too ...'

'What about Babs and Katie? Are you asking them?'

'Mam says I have to.' But I was in no hurry.

Paula's blue eyes looked sort of pleading in the mirror. 'Sarah, do you think Miranda would give Tanoli and me a jumping lesson while she's here?'

'I'm not sure how long she's staying. But I'll ask her.' Energetically finishing off with a few broad white streaks across her forehead and throwing down the brushes, I grabbed the blanket off the bed.

'Come on. We'd better practise our war dance.'

Outside, we went to the sally tree beside the rhubarb patch and Dad showed us how make a bow from a long thin sally branch, using the nylon string.

I threw the blanket over Bluebell's back and hopped up. 'You look terrific.' Dad opened the gate for us and Paula jogged alongside, carrying the bow and arrow.

Back home, after feeding Bluebell apples and crisps, I turned her out into her paddock to graze.

'Well, how'd you get on?' Dad was spooning the gravy over the roast meat. 'Did you do the war dance?'

'No. We didn't have to do anything. They gave us lots.'

'Any sign of Miranda?' Mam looked anxious, face all blotchy from the heat of the oven.

But Dad told her not to worry.

Back in my bedroom, after emptying the bags of goodies and dividing them, we started eating. There was a bar of Turkish Delight each, three Mars bars and a Bounty, apples, crisps and loads of nuts. I showed Paula my lip, where my cold sore was starting. I heard voices in the kitchen. Then Mam laughing. Loud music blaring. For some reason I felt like laughing too.

The bedroom door opened and there was Miranda. 'I had to walk up from the bus stop in the village. I'm dead.'

I couldn't help feeling happy about something as I watched her throw off her backpack and flick her battle sandals on to the floor. 'Move over.' She hitched up her long skirt and sat cross-legged on the bed beside me.

'Glad I'm here?'

I nodded. She was here and in a good mood and I didn't want to spoil anything. I just said, 'Mam was worried you mightn't come.'

She shrugged and adjusted her floppy hat.

Paula was busily wiping the make-up off her face and seemed embarrassed at Miranda seeing us with all the paint on our faces but I didn't care.

I peered under the hat, at Miranda's heavy eye make-up. 'Is that a mask you're wearing?'

'Maybe it is.' Miranda was still in a fun mood. She switched her voice and cackled like a witch, 'Maybe I'm not me. Maybe I'm just pretending to be me.'

We giggled, then I asked her how long she could stay.

'Have to be back the day after tomorrow.' Casually munching.

'But don't you have the whole week off?'

She said in an annoyed tone, 'You sound like my mother,' and then added softly, 'I had a chat with Bluebell on my way in. She looks lovely.'

I suddenly felt happy again. 'She's brilliant. She's going really well.'

'Good. I'll give you another lesson tomorrow.'

'Dad said we can use the field if we want, so long as we don't cut it up too badly.' Then I saw Paula making faces at me and I remembered to ask, 'And could Paula have a lesson too?'

'Sure.' She smiled over at Paula. 'Now, let's go out to the kitchen. Mom will need a bit of help. And I want to prepare my own dinner.'

'Gawd, yeah. Mam made a right mess of it last time.'

'I'd better go,' Paula said. 'See you tomorrow.'

Miranda said vaguely, 'Tomorrow? Oh yes, the lesson.'

'And your birthday,' I said. It slipped out then. 'I've got a present for you and Mam's got a cake and Dad's getting off early from work.'

She stared hard at me, the pupils of her eyes growing bigger and blacker as if she was going to get very angry. But she didn't. 'Really?' That's all she said.

In the kitchen she asked Mam where the vegetables were. But she didn't mention her birthday, as if it were of no interest to her. My cold sore was bruised and tingling.

Mam hovered nearby while Miranda cooked. 'Stock cube.' I searched in the press and found one. 'Chicken ... '

Miranda handed it back to me and searched for herself.
'Here we are.' She tossed the vegetable cube into the soup.
She was checking labels. Suddenly she gave a little scream
and grabbed the spoon from Mam. 'Don't stir it with that
spoon! You've just stirred the gravy with it.' Then she
smiled: 'Sorry about that.' She opened a tin of kidney
beans and put them into a saucepan, adding some curry
powder and thickening it with cornflour. 'That's my
protein.'

Later, she helped herself from the vegetable dish that I
passed to her and said, 'I'm fitting in a bit better. I'm not
such a faddy, am I? And you're having the food you like.'

'And you only used one small saucepan.'

She laughed. 'Sorry about all the washing-up you had to
do last time.'

Mam was smiling. 'You can come shopping with me
tomorrow. I still have things to get for the party ... '

Mam had been talking about Miranda's seventeenth
birthday for ages – as if no one ever had a birthday before.
One sure thing, she had never planned anything like it for
me. There was to be a big chocolate cake from Superquinn
as well as chocolate eclairs because Miranda loves eclairs.
She'd been told she could invited the McDonnells, her
friends, even Yaquob. Yet, one thing I couldn't understand.

'Mam, what present are you giving Miranda?' There had
been no mention of it. Maybe she was getting her a car or
something. Carmencita had got a car for her seventeenth
birthday.

There was a silence. Then Miranda said quickly, 'I don't
want anything.'

But Mam smiled mysteriously. 'Yes, I have got a birthday present for you, Miranda. It's very special.' Her voice
was very warm.

Well, as you know, Mam was good at keeping secrets.

Dad reminded Mam that they were supposed to be
going to the Naughtons' party.

'Do we have to?' Mam was looking sadly at Miranda.

Miranda said, 'Of course you'll go.' She turned to me. 'We'll be glad to be on our own, won't we, Sarah?'

I hardly noticed we were doing the washing-up and it was almost like fun because we were talking about horses and the different ones in the livery yard and what to do if an epidemic of strangles broke out in the yard and all that important stuff.

Then there was a loud knock at the door. It was Babs and Katie. Babs was wearing an old dress of her mother's and a devil's mask with horns on it. Katie's face was pitch-black and Babs said she'd put soot on it. We all took turns at fishing the five, ten and twenty pence coins from the basin of water. Water held no fear for Babs and her face stayed under the surface for as long as necessary. She and Katie were showing off in front of Miranda who ignored them.

'Heard you're having a party, Miranda.' Babs was dripping all over the place. 'Are we invited?'

had not worked. It was red and ugly-looking and had ruined my whole lip.

'I'm getting out of here.'

'You can't leave now, just when we're getting to know each other.' Mam was shouting.

'Isn't that exactly what you did seventeen years ago?'

'I had no choice.'

'You could have kept me.'

'It was different then.'

When the voices stopped, I slipped into the kitchen. It was empty and I picked up the crumpled note that lay on the floor. Back in my bedroom I opened and read it.

It was a letter and I recognised Mam's handwriting: 'Dearest Daughter Roisin ...' it began, '... I was young. I was on my own. I had no money. I wanted what was best for you at the time, the security of two parents. I miss you ... ' I stopped reading.

Mam lonely. Why couldn't she have told me?

Footsteps again and I quickly put the note away. It was Miranda. Her big floppy hat was back on and I couldn't see her face too well. She sounded calm. 'I have to go. I'll just gather my bits and pieces and be off. Your mother can't wait to be rid of me, I'm such a disruption. She needn't worry. I won't be bothering her any more.'

I said, 'Are we not your family any more then?'

'It's not that, Sarah. I told you, I'm confused. Now I have two families.'

'Here's your present.' Grandad's tenner had gone to very good use.

'Thanks.' She took it, then leaned over and hugged me. My cold sore was hurting so much I could hardly talk. I wanted to tell her that if she didn't like it she could take the box of acrylics back to the shop and exchange them for something else. Or for different colours. When I'd gone shopping with her that day I'd really have liked to have got her the telescopic tripod for her painting easel that I saw on the window, so that she could set it up anywhere and paint out in the field or at the seaside or somewhere and paint all day or even at night.

The sound of a car honking outside broke in on my thoughts. I remembered how I used to love that sound. I heard the front door slam, and after the car pulled away I waited until the house stopped rattling.

Her room was very silent. I smelled the new scent *Poison* that Mam had bought for her and the sweat from her runners mixed with the smell of cigarettes.

Bluebell's photo had stood on her locker top. It was gone. She'd asked me for it and I'd given it to her on her first day. It was taken during the summer and it showed Bluebell standing in the field of purple clover wearing her yellow tail bandage; it was my favourite photo of her. I was sitting in the saddle wearing my wine-coloured anorak, a pair of shorts over my jodhpurs and Bluebell's head was turned at an angle, so that her wall eye was looking at the camera and her tail was falling in a silver and yellow wave. Miranda must have taken it with her.

Something else caught my eye. Kneeling down I rooted in the waste-paper basket. What was that on the ground?

I sorted out the torn halves of the birthday card.

Back in my room I spent time fitting them together and then I sellotaped them. The picture of the princess with the three supporting pillars looked as good as new. Almost. The beautiful princess would never be the same. Her face was blurry where the torn halves did not fit properly together. Still ...

I trotted Bluebell the whole way to Paula's. Tanoli was in the stable and Paula told me I could let Bluebell graze in the garden. I'd just untacked when it started to rain. Paula and I sheltered under the roof overhang while it pelted down. Bluebell was getting very wet. She stood, head lowered, with her back to it. She was miserable.

After a few moments, Paula said, 'Will we try it?'

'Okay.'

I led Bluebell into the small stable with Tanoli. Tanoli looked at Bluebell and Bluebell looked at his hay. We closed the door on them. From outside we could hear quiet munching. Paula was frowning. She said, 'If that's Bluebell eating Tanoli's hay, he'll go mad.'

The half door was just above our eye level. We leaped up and down.

'God! Look!'

Tanoli was sharing his hay with her. They were munching together. Bluebell and Tanoli had made friends.

Later, in Paula's room, we ate some of Miranda's birthday cake. Paula rubbed at the smudge of chocolate on her duvet. 'She shouldn't have gone. Your mam will be lonely.'

'I know.'

When I got home, Mam was still sitting by the phone but when Dad came in she hurried out of the room and he followed.

I tuned into *Friends* on the television.

'... Those people have cared for her since she was a baby. She has two mothers. We must accept it. And two fathers. We can't replace the parents who reared her.'

The voices grew quieter and I went and got more cake. I thought, 'I'm going to be sick if I don't stop eating.'

I heard Mam say, 'I wanted her so much to be part of my life. Maybe the party was inappropriate. Maybe I shouldn't have interfered. I probably caused the row. Maybe it was too much for Miranda to handle, being suddenly pulled in two different directions. I should have phoned that social worker that time and got help from them, let it happen more gradually...'

I went out into the field. Would Bluebell ever see her friend Blackie again. Would I ever see Miranda again? And did I care? Mam cared. Friends came and then they went. But Dad seemed sure. 'She'll be back, of course she'll be back,' he'd said.

Bluebell blew her steamy breath in my face and licked

my hair until it was like glue. It wasn't my fault. Miranda should never have come. Then no one would miss her.

Later, in bed, I was awake when Mam came in.

'Good-night, Mam.'

Sighing, she kissed me and went out.

Footsteps came back to my bed and stopped. 'Dad, I need a hot-water bottle.'

He said cheerfully, 'I thought you were asleep. One hot-water bottle coming up.'

The bottle was against my feet, making them uncomfortably hot and I pushed it away.

'Dad ...' I could hear crying behind a closed door.

'Yes, little daughter.'

'Miranda ...' It was all her fault. Why did she have to come back into our family and make Mam so unhappy? 'Dad, can't you fix things?'

'It's between Miranda and her mother. They'll work this out together. We'll let them be. Leave them alone for a while. There's a lot of sorting out to be done and it's going to take time. This is not a serious row. In getting to know each other, there's many a hump and hollow, like you and Bluebell getting to know each other.'

I felt his mighty hand on my forehead smoothing it out. 'Let all your wandering thoughts seep away through the top of your head.' His hand was pressing all the thoughts and sounds out while he talked on and on in his boring voice that wore down the darkness and sent it scuttling away. My toes curled around the bottle again.

'Take your hand away now, Dad. Good-night, Dad.'

'Goodnight, little daughter.'

Last thing I heard was the familiar sound of Bluebell scratching herself against the rattley gate of the field.

15 GOING HUNTING

I repeated over and over again to myself what Gweena had just told me on the phone. Then I went and told Mam.

'She'll be collecting Strike at the horse hospital. Then she's calling here for me and Bluebell. The X-rays show that Strike's back is sound and she can hunt him on Sunday. And she's taking me and Bluebell hunting with her.'

It seemed like ages since Gweena first promised me and now it was about to happen.

'I'm not sure ... why can't you wait for the Junior Hunt?'

I rushed to the door to meet Dad as he came in.

'Whoa, now. Give me a chance. What's all this about?' scanning Mam's face.

After hearing the details, he said it was a chance for me that I might not get again. 'Besides,' now speaking to Mam reassuringly, 'Sarah isn't going to do anything dangerous. She knows her pony and I'm confident that the two of them together will be able to manage and do the right thing.'

'But you know how some of those people go berserk out hunting.' Mam's voice was not as sure. 'They wouldn't even notice a child rider if she crossed their path. They'd just as quickly ride over her ...'

'Don't forget,' Dad said, 'Gweena will be with her. I don't envisage any real problem. And, I'm taking you away for the weekend.'

We waited but Mam said nothing.

'So, that's settled,' Dad said briskly. 'I'd better go and change.'

But Mam was still standing there, biting her thumb, looking at the floor.

'Come on, Mam.' Outside in the stable I showed her how to prepare a pony for a hunt. Bluebell had got a bit hairy around the face so she had to be clipped around her jaws and her ears and her shaggy fetlocks. It didn't take long.

'Isn't she beautiful?' Dropping the scissors I stood back so that Mam could have a proper look.

'She has a strong head and neck.' Mam's voice was low.

'Yes. I love the way she sticks out her neck when she's trotting.'

'Like a goose.'

'Yeah, well, arched necks don't appeal to me much. Too artificial.'

I brushed while Mam fetched the saddle from the porch. She helped me tack up for the practice session. One last thing; I checked my pony's hooves. They were a bit long but not long enough for her to trip and one of the clinches was up. But the shoe should hold in place even over rough ground.

'Watch.' Out in the field, I showed Mam how placing a pole on the ground in front of the jump helped Bluebell's judgement.

First time, she jumped so high she jerked me out of the saddle. But next time, she neatly cleared the top pole. I explained to Mam how she was learning from experience. It was nice to have her to myself again.

Then I demonstrated an extended trot. Bluebell executed an excellent one, really stretching but beautifully restraining herself from cantering. Next, a collected canter, brought about with just the slightest touch of my heel.

We were back in the stable, watching Bluebell eat her first-crop hay. Mam sighed and suddenly, turning, put her arms around me and we hugged each other. It was quiet in the stable except for the soft sound of Bluebell munching and the sweet smell of hay.

'Won't you be careful when you go on that hunt and stick with Gweena all the time?' Her voice was muffled. 'You're growing so tall, I don't get a chance to cuddle you any more.' Suddenly she bristled. Angrily she strode over to the manger and fished something out of it, dangling it in front of my face.

'What's this?' she demanded.

As if she couldn't see for herself that it was one of Dad's tartan socks. I'd been using it to polish Bluebell's hooves. She always gets into such a fuss about nothing.

That night I laid out my clothes for the hunt: clean jodhpurs, jacket, and stock with my new tie-pin and gloves. I cleaned and polished my boots. It was too late to polish my tack. That could be done when I got to Grandad's.

Dad stood with his hands in his pockets. There was no point in him fussing over the pony. He went to pick up the brush to brush Bluebell's tail. 'Leave it, Dad.' I told him to get the tack, all of it, and load it into the jeep. Also the boots and bandages.

Bluebell walked up the ramp and stood beside Strike who sniffed at the strange pony. Almost straightaway they nuzzled noses.

Dad lifted the ramp and Gweena climbed up into the jeep. She grasped the wheel. 'Right. We'll go.' Start up.

Tack box, head-collar, hay net, saddle and bridle. Hat, clean boots, shirt, stock, jodhpurs, gloves, jacket. I went over the list again in my mind to make sure I had forgotten nothing. Gweena didn't like people who were sloppy about their riding gear.

It felt kind of weird driving off in the jeep, leaving Mam and Dad and Paula waving by the roadside. It would have been great if Paula could have come too.

Still, I was lucky to get going at all. Gweena had said Grandad was not happy about me hunting with the Galways. I was glad Mam and Dad hadn't heard. They might have changed their minds about letting me go.

Gweena drove fast. As we sped along on the N6 she tapped her fingers on the wheel in time to Led Zeppelin's 'Babe, I'm gonna leave you' on the stereo. I loved the beat of the drums. She lowered the volume now and then and we listened for any disturbance in the trailer. But Strike and Bluebell were quiet. No argument between them back behind us so far.

'Sarah, you're now one hundred miles from Griffeen.'

My worries had vanished. 'I'm not scared about to-morrow.' My leg was whacking off the floor of the cab.

'That's good,' she yelled. 'As children we were always falling off our ponies and breaking bones. No harm.'

'Your horse could do a massive jump.'

She smiled. 'Yes. He has the power.' She told me to open the dashboard. 'You will need to know what to do when you get to the hunt.'

I took out the sheet and read through the list of Dos and Don'ts when out hunting.

Concentrate: better not walk on the hounds when hacking on the road; make sure I keep to the headlands when I'm in wheat; pray my pony isn't too restive around the hounds when they're casting around for the scent. I have to make way for the huntsman and hounds when they're trying to get through and pass on the word or shout 'Huntsman' or 'Hounds'. I must go around stock in the fields and not go through them and frighten them and if I'm last through the gate I must close it. Doff my cap? Oh, only for men and boys. And I must remember to thank the Master for a good day's sport when I'm going home.

Gweena shouted, 'Okay?'

'Yeah. Fine.' I put back the sheet.

I felt confident. I remembered what Niall told me about the time he went on an adult hunt. And how his pony was excited and he was so excited, he never thought of falling off or being afraid. I like Niall. He doesn't pretend he's the greatest, like Trevor.

I woke as we pulled up outside Grandad's. He was standing in the open doorway. Hurrying down the pathway to meet us as we got out, his stick lifted in a salute. 'Ye left it very late. Had ye any trouble?'

'What kind of trouble did you expect?' Gweena asked abruptly.

He moved into position beside the ramp, Suki on the alert beside him.

'Gweena, I don't know if it's wise to take this child huntin' ... '

Gweena didn't seem to hear him. She led Bluebell down the ramp and thrust her lead rope at me. 'Be ready at ten o'clock. I'll call for you.' She drove off in a hurry.

Grandad was not in his usual chatty form. On the way up to the orchard, he said crossly, 'Gweena is going off huntin' tomorrow. Wouldn't you think she'd stay at home and look after her husband and little child? She's gone every day. It's nothin' only horses, horses with her. If I left this place to Sam, she'd have it flooded with them.'

'But, Grandad, she has to hunt Strike if she's going to point-to-point him this year.'

'What!' Grandad almost stood on Suki and Bluebell jerked up her head in surprise. 'She's goin' racin'! That woman will get killed. What'll happen to her family then!'

Luckily we'd reached the field gate because Grandad's face was as red as a fire from his blood pressure.

'You're tired,' said Granny. 'You should be in bed with a big day ahead of you tomorrow. I'll give you a hot-water bottle and your blanket is on.'

'What's the hurry?' Grandad waved her away. 'Leave the child alone. She goes to bed far too early at home, that's why she's growing too tall.'

'I won't leave her alone.' Granny shushed him up. 'Remember she has to get up early in the morning.'

Grandad turned to me. 'Take no notice of that woman. She never stops talkin'. Are you warm there? Shove down to the fire. Now, tell me more about Bluebell. I might go to the hunt with ye tomorrow if I'm feelin' up to it. That pony turned inside out since I last saw her. She's a fine pony. And you're a fine little rider. The best I've seen for a long time. I'd love to see you up there with the hounds. I suppose Lady Molly will be out. She's not worth a damn to ride a horse and never was. But her father was the best man I ever saw to hunt hounds. Not like Paddy Egan, the eejit … Now, what were we talking about? Granny, what do you want now? Go out.'

I got up. 'Grandad, I still have to clean my tack.'

I followed Granny out to the kitchen. Spreading my tack on the floor I checked it for safety. The girth and buckles were sound. No sign of ripping in the stitching in the leather. Then I started into the polishing.

It was late before I got to bed but it still took ages for me to go to sleep. My leg kept me awake; it was hopping like crazy. I hoped Bluebell would behave at the hunt and wouldn't be bucking and kicking. And what about the other horses? How would they behave with her? They mightn't like her and lash out at her, like at Pony Camp.

What if she failed to jump the fences? What if she fell?

And what would happen if *I* fell off? How could I stand up again and face the crowd?

I collected the bedclothes off the floor and got back in. One thing I *could* do; I could make sure my pony looked nice. I would get up early and plait her mane even though Gweena said there was no need, that it was just a farmers' hunt.

Before my own breakfast I fed Bluebell with oats and hay and water. I couldn't finish my flakes, I felt so sick. Then it was back up to the shed to groom and plait her. When we arrived at the front gate of the house, Granny came out to meet us with chocolate bars and sprinkled holy water to keep us safe.

Gweena was there on time. I could see Strike's bandaged dock above the top of the ramp as she pulled up on the footpath in front of us.

She led Bluebell into the horse-box beside Strike who was fidgeting, moving from leg to leg. We were about to drive away, when I saw an orange-coloured tea-cosy at the upstairs window. The top sash fell down and Grandad's whiskery face peered through the opening.

'Bye, Grandad!'

He shouted, 'Gweena, mind that innocent child. That's rough country out there and it's full of barbed wire. Don't let her out of your sight. And keep her away from those hooligans ...!'

The rest of what he had to say was buried in the loud revving of the engine.

Sheep grazed on sparkling grey grass in the small stone-walled fields.

'Where's the hunt meeting?' My knee was tapping like a drumstick, vibrating the dashboard and Gweena's brown leather riding-gloves and navy velvet riding-hat. I put my hand on it to steady it.

'You'll see.' She slowed down. Her grumpy look was gone. She smoothed the front of her green tweed jacket and checked her stock in the mirror. 'There's been a change of plan.' She explained that because some farmers had refused permission to the hunt to ride through their lands the Master would have to change the route.

'Don't worry. You won't be disappointed. You'll come across some fine jumps for Bluebell today.' Airily she waved a hand at walls and ditches on each side as we drove along. 'This will be a much better hunt than any of the hunts around Dublin. You'll have something to tell your friends about when you get home, don't you worry.' She pushed the long gear handle forward and backward and slowed at bends. A rider on horseback came into view. Then another and another.

'Here we are.'

We pulled up behind a lorry near the black gates. I rolled down the window and looked in among the headstones. A couple of bicycles were lying against the graveyard wall. Horse-boxes and lorries and pick-up trucks and go-carts were parked on the verge of the road.

Gweena said not to unload yet. She put on Strike's bridle, then took off his travelling rug and tail bandage and I did the same with Bluebell. They needed time to get used to the atmosphere, she said.

Anyway, Bluebell was in no hurry. She stopped, looked around and whinnied before walking down the ramp. Not so Strike. We just got out of the way. Bursting out of the trailer as if it were full of a pack of devils he tried to break loose and it took all Gweena's strength to hold him.

'You won't need the spurs today, Gweena!' someone shouted.

She roared at Strike and he quietened. But she decided to use the martingale, which would help keep his head down and give her better control.

I had Bluebell fully tacked up now and she looked smart with her plaited mane and tail, all fluffy after being brushed. Beside her, Strike looked splendid with the black bandages decorating his front legs and matching black numnah.

Gweena stepped up on a boulder. 'Whoa. Steady!' Strike was pulling away from her.

I remembered how Strike had responded so dutifully to Henry the huntsman at Punchestown. 'Will Henry be riding with us today?' I asked Gweena.

'No. He's gone to Kildysart to look at a horse for Bob. The Master will be acting as huntsman for the day.' She put her foot into the stirrup and sprang into the saddle and I did the same.

The hunt had grouped on a grassy verge further along by the wall. I rode Bluebell forward to let her see and smell the others and get to know them. But she didn't seem too surprised by all the horses and riders and her strange surroundings and behaved in her usual well-mannered way.

Probably she was pleased to be away from Strike for the moment. He was all fussed up, kicking out and bucking on the road. The old lady who sat side-saddle on a big bay horse let out a sudden roar as he backed into her. But Gweena spoke to him in a calm and firm voice and continued to circle him. I moved Bluebell out of the way to make room for Stan, the thin loopy rider I had seen at Punchestown. He wore a pink coat over black tights and runners. Gweena said he was whipper-in for the day. The rider beside him was wearing a shiny pinstripe suit, the legs tucked into rubber boots. A boy of about my own age rode towards us but I kept Bluebell far away from his skittish piebald pony.

Strike seemed more settled now. Gweena flicked a dry leaf off her glove and smiled at us as we came over. 'How's it going? We should be moving off soon.' She looked happy and at ease. She was out to enjoy the day.

I tried to relax too. But I couldn't help messing with the reins and it was making Bluebell nervous. She stopped

tossing her head and watched fascinated at the hounds pouring out of the red van. I kept her facing them in case she'd get a mad fright if they swarmed under her legs. The other riders and horses didn't seem to mind.

The Master rode towards us with his cap outstretched and Gweena rooted in her pocket.

'Well, good hunting.' He slipped the money into his pocket and grandly doffed his cap to me.

There was a roar. 'Donnelly, blow the horn.'

But Donnelly didn't blow as ordered because he couldn't find the hunting-horn and the hunt moved off without him. Bluebell had cooled down now that Strike was with us, although the big chestnut was all jittery. I let him go on ahead of me. Pulling with his head, he exploded into short gallops, steaming and crashing into horses that were bottle-necked on the narrow road.

I was trying to make sure that we didn't get crushed by the other riders pressing in from all sides of us. I wanted

Bluebell to have enough room to move freely and not get hemmed in. Other horses were frisking about in an excitable state, but Bluebell seemed not fussed at all by the strange sights or sounds or movements. She was as steady as the bough of an oak tree under me.

'They're going to try Ballymoss covert.' Pointing to clumps of furze several fields away, Gweena reined in beside us. Her smile showed cool excitement.

She was taking good care of me now. Whenever Strike tried to break away, she circled him skilfully and waited for us to catch up. The leaders were trotting and Strike went skittering all over the road wanting to be in front with them. Bluebell ambled meekly along behind him. Our breaths and the breaths of the horses made small fogs in the air.

'Why did the farmers not allow us to hunt through that valley there?'

'They have their reasons.'

A sudden movement by Strike threw Gweena forward in the saddle. 'Whoa. Easy, boy.' The big heavy horse crushed in beside Bluebell again and I just managed to lift my leg clear.

I patted my placid pony. Still, Gweena seemed to be enjoying her horse's friskiness. She was an excellent horsewoman.

'That farmer is always grumbling. What he doesn't know won't trouble him.'

For some reason, an orange tea-cosy floated into my head, then out quickly again.

We all rode down a boreen, but we were delayed at a place where the wall of the field was broken down. The leading horses jumped over the untidy heap of stones in turn but some were refusing. Not so Strike. Forcing the other horses out of his way, he lunged over it and there Gweena halted, her strong hands holding him in check.

Bluebell didn't like the look of those loose stones and neither did I. But she picked her way over them and we galloped down the field after the others.

There was a deep gully, flanked by a high ditch. One by one, with much pushing, the horses scrambled in and out and over. Left behind were Bluebell and me and the other junior rider on the piebald pony. Unflustered, Bluebell looked from the big ditch back at me.

I slipped off her back and took the reins. 'Come on, Bluebell.' I tugged hard. With a little hop, she followed and together we slid down the slope. I jumped across the gully and she jumped alongside. I scrambled up the mound with the help of a sapling and she followed and jumped into the next field. The boy and his pony had disappeared.

We galloped on again and caught up with the end of the hunt at the next ditch. But, again, Bluebell baulked and I went to lead her across. She stood, stubbornly resisting at first, then took a sudden leap that unbalanced me and I slithered into her path. Luckily she hopped clear over me.

Phew! We were just a bit muddy.

I could see the other riders galloping towards the pine plantation. Gweena had given Strike his head. He whizzed over the low wall and Bluebell and I came after him. We were clear. Maybe Bluebell was getting into the swing of things. We cantered through the sedgy meadow. Gweena has already overtaken some of the others at the river. Horses and riders were scrambling through it with difficulty. I wheeled Bluebell to the left and led her through the gate. A few other horses went through before I bolted it shut.

The hunt had already entered the forest. But Bluebell was in no hurry on the incline and we went along at a nice easy canter. At the edge of the forest, I could make out some hoofmarks in the gap in the fence but there was no sight or sound of the hunt. Bluebell whinnied for Strike, but got no answer.

We walked and trotted along by the forest boundary until we got to a roadway. Just then I heard the sound of the hunting-horn. Great! Gweena and the others were not far away. A horse and rider trotted past us and went on down the road. 'They're gone on – to Clooniffe.'

Bluebell's interest was in grazing. I flapped the reins and she moved forward slowly. I wished I had my spurs.

She started when a horse and rider scrambled through the bushes and jumped on to the road in front of us. Blood trickled down the pony's right leg and the boy was cursing. 'The stupid animal ran into barbed wire,' he shouted to a man who had leaped from his car. 'He nearly killed me, Da.'

'Get down.' Grabbing at the bridle, his father examined the cut, then quickly undid the girth. 'That's your huntin' over for today, me man.'

We heard the hooves coming and I yanked Bluebell out of the way. Strike cleared the ditch. Gweena spun him on a tight rein and he left a trail of froth on the road.

She called out to me, 'Where have you been? I've been searching all over ... You go home with Jamesy.'

'But I want to do the hunt ... '

'That pony can't hunt.' Her cheeks were flushed, her face and eyes full of danger and excitement. Twisting Strike about, she shouted to the boy's father, 'Jamesy, can you give them a lift back to Gurteen, to her grandfather's?'

'Dinny Quinn's is it? She's welcome to be sure.' Jamesy was trying to keep his distance from Strike. He broke off. 'Pon me oath ... that's some dynamo. There's enough electricity in him to light up the whole County Galway,' wiping the froth off his ear.

'But I don't want to go home ... '

'Tell your father to get you a right pony.'

Gweena and Strike were gone. The last I saw of them they were galloping with the others towards the river.

16 GOING HOME

As Strike and Gweena sped down the slope, I looked down at my pony chomping grass by the roadside and felt a huge disappointment and anger. Bluebell couldn't hunt and she'd never make a hunter. She'd never make a show-jumper. She was never going to be a champion. I flung the reins on to the pummel of the saddle. 'You're no friend. You're a disgrace.'

I'd been fooling myself all along. My once best friend Babs was right about her. Bluebell had a disease – a disease of laziness. She just was not a pony to fly across country and ditches and keep up with hounds like the fiery Strike. He was magic!

'Come on, you lazyboots.' We were going home. I was to meet Jamesy at the pub down the road.

I could see over the low wall down into the valley. The distant 'Oi Oi Oi Oi' of the hounds drifted up and sometimes I glimpsed a few horses dashing about in a clearing among the trees and bushes.

In the silent little grove where we were standing, a hazel tree shed a nut and it fell into Bluebell's mane. It was a mugar-le-muire, a very unusual nut like a Siamese twin – Grandad had one in the jeep. Bluebell looked up and cocked her ears fully. I chucked roughly at her mouth. Her loud whinny of protest vibrated through me.

'I've had enough of this.' She started again at the anger in my voice. 'You're the laziest pony in all of Ireland. I'm ashamed of you.'

She cocked her head sharply. But I could see her attention was elsewhere now. She wasn't listening to me.

She was really very alert for the first time today. I dried my eyes and my face and we went down the road towards the pub. But the car park of the pub was empty. Jamesy had said he wouldn't go without us. Where was he?

A fat man in a waistcoat answered the door. 'You mean Jamesy and Joe? They're all gone to Clooniffe. There's a horse in trouble there.' He pointed to a grassy boreen. 'It's not very far. You can't miss them.'

I needed no spurs now. Bluebell was very eager and I had to keep a tight rein to stop her from cantering. We hopped over the bushes in the gap into the field. Over by the limestone wall, riders had dismounted and they stood with their horses in a half-circle.

The woman rider stood by the gate. Her face was white and her breeches were muddied. There was a fluttery feeling in my stomach. 'Gweena, where's Strike?'

She didn't look at me. I rode closer and in the hollow near the gate I saw the horse lying stretched on the grass. A beautiful chestnut horse. His soft brown eyes looked up at me. Strike was quiet as he breathed deeply, his sides sucking in and out.

'The vet is coming. Keep back there.' As Bluebell moved in to smell Strike, the man caught her roughly by the bridle. 'Take yourself and your pony out of here. This is no place for you.'

Gweena's head was bowed, her chin resting on her chest.

'What's wrong with Strike?'

'His neck is broken. The vet will shoot him.' She walked away.

Low voices. 'A double somersault over that big wrought-iron gate.'

'It's amazing the woman wasn't killed.'

The fat man was standing at the front door of the pub. 'Any news?'

'Which is the road to Gurteen?' I wanted to get to Grandad's house.

'It's a good bit from here. Turn left ...' Calling after me, 'What way is that horse?'

Bluebell and I set off at a brisk pace up the empty road. We turned off at the junction where the signpost read: 'Gurteen 10 miles.'

I wasn't worried. Bluebell had done a ten-mile hack before and she was still fresh. Although we didn't know our way, we'd probably meet up with others from the hunt.

Bluebell heard the recoil before I did. The skin on her neck flickered. She stopped, ears pricked to the echo of the faint sound that sent the crows cawing and scattering overhead.

'It's okay, Bluebell.' Patting her, my hand shook. After a few moments she plodded on again.

I felt so sad for the beautiful horse that was dead.

The patter of Bluebell's hooves on the road. Going on and on. There were no houses and no traffic, just land and bog on each side with furze bushes and heather. We were climbing the winding hill along by the conifer plantation. What time was it? My watch – I realised I'd forgotten to put it on this morning.

I was getting tired and let the reins slip loose but Bluebell kept going on at a regular pace. Another junction with a signpost. Oh, no, we must have taken a wrong turning. The signpost read: 'Gurteen 14 miles' ... but which way?

Bluebell showed no interest in the sign but went on purposefully. I tried to figure out what to do. No panic. Maybe we should double back the way we came. Or would we save time by cutting through that plantation, and maybe meet up with the hunt?

It was gloomy in among the trees. Bluebell kept her pace, seemingly comforted by the cushioned ground under her hooves. The sweet peppermint smell of the pine needles reminded me of the chocolate bar Granny gave me and I felt its chunky shape in my pocket.

It was deadly still now, except for a small stream tinkling over stones. Then a brownish cat appeared and played around us. Was it friendly or did it want to scrape or bite Bluebell? But Bluebell showed no fear and kept going forward on the narrow pathway. In the soft wet darkness pencils of light coming through showed it was still bright outside. 'Good girl,' patting her. I was sure she'd find her way. I listened for sounds of the hunt but heard only the muffled sound of Bluebell's hooves on the brown needles and the sharp clink of her shoe.

Coming out of the forest on to a narrow road I heard the clink-clonk again so I got off and examined her hooves. Amazingly, three of her shoes were missing. The remaining hind shoe was swinging loose. I'd have to get it off. The shoe could pivot on the nail and the quarter clips would dig into the frog, making her lame. After levering it off I felt tired and sat down for a rest on a mossy rock. Bluebell lifted her head suddenly.

The evening brightness glinted on rocks and hard grass and a cold breeze blew across my face. We were on the side of a mountain. Suddenly I felt lost. Grandad's house and Gurteen could be fifty miles away from here.

Bluebell's ears were still focused firmly forward.

'I'd better eat my bar.' Her ears swung back for an instant as if she was listening. I gave her a square and she nuzzled me for more. 'Not now.'

Seeing the lights coming towards us in the distance, I leaped to my feet. 'Someone's coming.' But Bluebell showed no interest. The Hiace van stopped beside us and I could see the fiery bob of a piebald pony sticking out through the front of the open-topped trailer it was pulling. The driver rolled down the window.

'Lady, we'd give you a good price for that pony.' His red eyes slithered up and down Bluebell.

'This pony is not for sale.' My voice sounded strong.

But they kept staring and grinning out at us.

I mounted as fast as I could and Bluebell set off through

the rushes. The men's laughter changed to shouts. 'Come back ...' Their calls grew fainter until they vanished into the swishing of the wind in the purple night grass we were walking through. The mushy ground heaved under us.

The perspiration on my body had turned to ice. I was wearing my vest, my shirt, Uncle Sam's body protector and my riding-jacket and I tried to close my anorak over them. 'Oh, no.' The zip was stuck. The wind had whipped my tie out. But all the layers underneath would probably have burst it anyhow.

My tummy felt as if someone was scraping it inside. I fingered the remains of my 10% extra Mars bar again. Huge rocks and holly trees rose up before us. Without a landmark I had no idea of where we were going.

But Bluebell walked on with a purposeful, eager pace, skirting pools, climbing over springy heather and stepping across grassy patches, showing no signs of tiredness. At least those men in the van wouldn't be able to find us now.

The clouds swirled about the moon making shadows. It was dark. It was now up to Bluebell to take us through safely. A sudden flutter of wings from a turf bank made her shy and I nearly fell into the glittering water. But like lightning she corrected her course and resumed her controlled pace. Full of courage, she gave me courage too.

At one point she was moving through mud and it seemed to be rising up to her knees, sucking at us, yet she still ploughed forward. Even when I desperately tried to rein her to the right, she wouldn't yield. Reaching the higher ground, in the reflected light I realised that I had been steering her into a shadowy cut-away bog.

The moon was a sleepy gold. I had taken my feet out of the stirrups so as to keep them free of the black butter. The rain came down, slow plops at first. My pony's rhythm was steady and swift through the slanting rain. Next thing, I lay on my back on something soft and moving. Bluebell's sour breath blew in my face, reviving me. Her mighty teeth, like Dad's vice grips, were clutching at my jacket.

Somehow I was in the saddle again.

I can't tell you because I can't remember how many times Bluebell breathed her warm sour breath into my face and nudged me up off the spongy turf when I wanted to rest.

And then, she came to a halt. We were not going forward any more and were sheltered from the cold and rain. Sliding off Bluebell my hand pressed against crusty turf walls. But it felt sort of cosy and warm – a turf cave. I lay down on mossy bumpy sods with Bluebell standing over me. Every time I woke, the wind and rain sounded in the distance like the scraggy trees of Grandad's house. I dreamt I was stacking bales of straw with him in the lean-to shed, falling between them and staggering up again.

The ground stirred under me. Bluebell shook herself in the dim light. It was dawn. My toes were freezing and my knees stiff. I got to my feet and, looking down, saw only a greeny-brown wilderness. Sedge and white bog cotton waved on the sweep of bog-land and I heard the calling of a snipe and the wind crying around the broken-down house of sods where we had spent the night.

Bluebell's legs were coated with peat up to her shoulders and brown muck was spattered on her white blaze. I was black mud everywhere: coat, jodhpurs, knickers, jumper, cap, gloves. When I used a tissue on my cheeks, it was black. I finished my chocolate while Bluebell nibbled the tough grass.

'We'd better move on, Bluebell. People will be looking for us.'

I crawled out of the turf bank and up into the saddle and Bluebell, sure as ever, set off at a strong jog. We moved at a squelchy rhythm through the drizzle; it felt like walking on a sponge in the shower. On and on.

Bluebell stood on the stony boreen biting blades of grass. This time I was wide-awake. The sunlight was reflected off the wet rocks and tufts of rushes. We were safely out of the bog.

My feet and legs were still numb and I didn't feel able to walk. But, again, Bluebell knew what to do. She opened the gate with her mouth and, pushing through, she trotted off with fresh determination.

'Bluebell! Look!'

Above the clump of furze bushes rose a white wisp of smoke. As we came nearer I could see the stone-slated roof.

Bluebell quickened her pace. Down the track towards the cottage to the sound of the squelching saddle. She was in a hurry. Side-stepping and tossing her head, wishing for her freedom. I saw small windows, red-berried holly trees at each gable.

From our right came the muffled sound of hooves and an excited lowing. Then a strange thing happened. Across the bog-land towards us came a black bullock, then another and another, long horns curving above their heads.

Bluebell stood to attention and gave one long, loud, trumpeting whinny. The sound exploded over the valley and echoed off the boulders, vibrating through the bog-lands and releasing the trapped air bubbles. This new energy seemed to seep into my pony and she started to prance, stepping out like never before. I was clinging to the mane. Clouds of snort collected about us. Her head was up, still searching. She moved forward in an extended trot. Then she halted and stood erect to the sound of the long answering whinny.

Trotting up to us came a shaggy grey mare.

Then I heard a voice. An old woman was standing in the open doorway.

'Well, Glory be to God, Bartley, c'mere quick. Miffy's foal is outside. And there's a little black craythur ... '

I could feel myself sliding.

' ... there, there, a *chuid*. I'll ... '

17 ENDINGS AND BEGINNINGS

A strong whiff of wet dog.

'That pony is so sure-footed, she'd take you safely from here to Clifden – no bother to her.' Grandad was peering at me, mouth open, glasses winking. 'Something told me this is where I'd find the two of them...'

'Where's Bluebell?' My voice sounded far away.

Grandad was smiling at the old man. '... and that the pair of them would be safe – Bluebell is in the back kitchen, eatin' all round her. Now, you drink that.' He handed me a big mug of sweet milky tea. 'Well, begod ... '

He sat back. 'Do you know what I'm going to tell ye,' looking from the old couple and back to me, 'that's the best little pony – in Ireland! You wouldn't meet the likes of her anywhere. A wonderful animal. You wouldn't meet the likes of her ... ' waving his stick at the mountain outside, ' ... in the whole of Arabia. That's breeding for you.'

'True for you, Mr Quinn. You're after a fair night of it yoursel', searchin' around the mountain ... '

The old woman added, 'Have a sup of tay.'

I yawned a long deep yawn.

That brought Grandad to his feet. He nodded to the old man. 'I'll be back in a while for the pony.'

Roaring down the boreen in the jeep, Bluebell who was grazing behind the low wall with her mother sprang into life. She galloped alongside, tail up. Her mother and the cattle were chasing behind in a wild burst of freedom. But when she came to the wall she swung around and legged it back up again towards the cottage.

I knew she was glad to be back where she was born.

'They're going all over the country, searching for you. Your father and mother and Miranda,' Grandad was yelling above the roar of the engine. 'The Clare side of the Slieve Aughties they went, the wrong direction altogether! Something was telling me all night that Bluebell would head for where she knew ye'd be safe. You know, I told them that. "Bluebell will head for Bartley's as sure as there's a bill on a duck." You can't beat nature!'

Grandad was right. Last night I became aware that Bluebell's strengths and capabilities were there before I met her. I hadn't taught her. She'd got them from Miffy her mother and her father and from living here on the mountain until she was three years old.

I thought of Miranda and knew now why it was so important for her to find her mother. And I knew too that I had many things to discover about myself yet. My leg gave a tiny hop with excitement.

'I hope you weren't too worried about me last night, Grandad.'

'Me worried! Not at all! I never worry. Now, Granny was worried. But Granny is awake every night.'

We were out on the main road now. 'Miranda ... there's great nature in her. She thought she could pick up your trail. She's fond of you.

He was saying something about a painting of Bluebell done by Miranda, as real as ever he'd seen.

I thought: Miranda did a painting of Bluebell. So that's why she took my photograph. And what about Gweena? Did she have photographs of her horse?

'Did they bury Strike?'

The jeep swerved and Grandad mumbled, 'Now, now ... we'll not talk about that today ...'

'Your pony smelled her home place from across the mountain, you see.' He was shouting again above the noise of the engine. 'She's a wonderful little pony. She's ... a ... she's a best friend.'

EPILOGUE

I'm in bed. There's a fire in the grate which Dad says hasn't been lit since he was a child dying of pneumonia. The smoke has cleared in the room, now that Grandad has carried off the jackdaw's nest in the bucket.

Miranda is switching from Fifth to Transition Year at school and she's going to use some of the time to go on a student exchange in Italy. Mam and Dad and the McDonnells are encouraging her to do this. They think she needs the extra year before she sits her Leaving Cert exam, seeing as this year has been traumatic for her and she hasn't been able to concentrate on doing proper homework, or anything. And what better place than Italy? She'll need to do loads more sketches and stuff to flesh out her portfolio for getting into Art College later on. There's even talk of me visiting her there during the hols.

Someone's banging on the window. Gazing in at me from under the hedge in Bluebell, fully groomed, looking radiant. Maybe I'll get to do a round of the field with her before the sun goes down.

Miranda gave me a leg up. 'Sorry about the party,' she said. 'I ruined it for all of you.'

What party? 'No problem,' I told her.

Bluebell reached back to scratch her sleek and bulging belly and gently planted greeny slime on my toes.

Miranda laughed. 'I like having a younger sister.'

I like having an older sister.

But it *is* weird.

128